THE MARBLE ORCHARD

Fiction by William F. Nolan

William F. Nolan

THE MARBLE ORCHARD

A Novel Featuring
The Black Mask Boys:

DASHIELL HAMMETT,
RAYMOND CHANDLER,
AND
ERLE STANLEY GARDNER

ST. MARTIN'S PRESS   NEW YORK

Design by Basha Zapatka

Library of Congress Cataloging-in-Publication Data

Nolan, William F.
    The marble orchard : a black mask boys mystery featuring Raymond Chandier / William F. Nolan.
      p.   cm.
    "A Thomas Dunne book."
    ISBN 0-312-14011-8
    1. Gardner, Erle Stanley, 1889–1970—Fiction. 2. Hammett, Dashiell, 1894–1961—Fiction. 3. Chandler, Raymond, 1888–1959—Fiction. 4. Authors, American—20th century—Fiction. 5. Murder—California, Southern—Fiction. 6. California, Southern—Fiction.
    I. Title.
PS3564.O39M37   1996
813'.54—dc20   95-45270
                                         CIP

First edition: January 1996

10 9 8 7 6 5 4 3 2 1

This one is for

JOE GORES

Friend,
Fellow Detectivist,
and the Father of Fictional Hammetts.

Thanks, Joe!

When I finally croak, and they plant me in the marble orchard with all the other stiffs, just make sure my tombstone says: "He was one tough monkey."

—ascribed to Al Capone, circa 1930s

Narrated by Raymond Chandler

ONE

Murder has always fascinated me. What impels one human being to take the life of another? What was the killer's state of mind at the time of the murder? Exactly how was the murder committed? In what circumstances and under what conditions? What was the motive? Was it a crime of passion or was it planned in advance with calculated malice? What clues have emerged during the investigation? If the killer's identity is unknown then will he, or she, ever be brought to justice?

Take last year's case of screen comedienne Thelma Todd. On the morning of December 16, 1935, her body was discovered slumped behind the wheel of her Lincoln Phaeton convertible in a closed garage above the ocean highway on Posetano Road. A sample of her blood revealed a saturation level of seventy percent carbon monoxide, and when she was found that morning the garage still reeked of engine fumes. The homicide dicks dubbed it a suicide—despite the fact that Todd's body bore the marks of a savage beating. Her blonde hair was streaked with blood, her nose was broken, and she had two cracked ribs.

Reading about the case in the *Times* last December didn't surprise me. The police were being well paid to ignore the truth about Todd's death. It wasn't suicide, it was murder.

A few people on the inside suspected Thelma's ex-husband, Pat DiCicco. He was known to have a violent temper, and had used his fists on Thelma more than once during the course of their brief, combative marriage. Also, he was the last person she was seen with on the night of her death. He wasn't satisfied with his end of the divorce; he wanted a share in Thelma's place, The Sidewalk Cafe.

But I didn't buy DiCicco as the killer. It was obvious to me that the man behind Todd's death was gangster Charles "Lucky" Luciano, who'd been into Thelma's pants for the past two years. She was a fast stepper (the press called her "Hot Toddy") and had always been attracted to lowlifes. Luciano is as low as they come. His West Coast "business interests" include prostitution, gambling, and drugs—and his attempt to cut himself a large slice of the Hollywood pie is well known within the industry.

Things had gone sour between Lucky and his hot-blooded lady love. Luciano tried to hook her on drugs to soften her up for a proposition. He wanted to lease the third floor of her cafe as a gambling casino. She had refused. Nothing he could say would change her mind.

Thelma was no sap. She knew that Lucky was not a man to say "no" to—not if you valued your health. But she figured he loved her enough to accept her decision. She figured wrong.

To me, the scenario was clear. Lucky has some tough lads working for him: "Icepick Lou" Stresh from Baltimore, "Kid Lobo" from El Paso, "Southpaw Willie" Grimes out of Georgia, and Chicago's pride and joy, Eddie Lasher, who's big enough to earn his nickname, "The Gorilla." "I like to squeeze 'em," he says, and the crushed windpipes of his victims attest to his unsavory preference. Any one of these boys could have taken care of little Thelma, and it was my guess one of them did.

Lucky left L.A. right after the "suicide." Figured it wouldn't be smart to stick around town. It was now mid-April, four months since Todd's death, and spring in Southern California, but that cold Pacific fog continued to roll in every morning before the sun had a whack at it, and I kept the fur collar of my Burberry topcoat turned up to ease the chill. It was just after dawn and the sky was still a sullen gray.

I was standing on the pavement directly in front of the two-car garage where Thelma's body had been found, at the juncture of Posetano Road and Stretto Way in the Palisades. This was an affluent area, with large, sprawling, Spanish-style houses dotting the hillsides at staggered intervals. Banker-doctor-lawyer country.

The garage was padlocked. Its two brass-studded wooden doors were separated by a cement post, and there was a small apartment above it, also Spanish-style, with a terra-cotta tile roof.

A thick swirl of milk-white fog obscured the brush- and weed-covered hillside above me. Below, at beach level, the ocean was sending in its usual heavy artillery; the faint boom of incoming surf against shoreline rocks was muted, part of another world. Up here, at the death site, I felt isolated, cut off from civilized society.

I was absorbing the atmosphere of murder. I was standing where Thelma's killer had stood after he'd closed the garage door on this savagely beaten woman. Did he experience any small degree of guilt or remorse? Did he regret his actions, even slightly? No, not him. This boy was a pro, and he probably enjoyed pulling off his little chore for the boss. Punching out a dumb jane, then dumping her into the Lincoln and starting the engine. Listening to that sweet purr of deadly exhaust. Grinning as he eased the garage door closed. Neat and simple. A job well done.

I shivered, and not just from the fog; this kind of calculated murder was chilling to think about. Huddled into my coat, I walked along Posetano Road for approximately a thousand feet, to the damp row of cement steps leading down to Thelma's Side-walk Cafe, two hundred and seventy of them, flanked by iron handrails as cold as a pimp's soul.

As part of their "investigation," the cops claimed that Todd had climbed these steps during the night to reach her car. Yet the maid who found her, Mae Whitehead, was on record as saying that Thelma was wearing a new pair of party shoes. If she *had* climbed those rough cement steps the soles would have been badly scuffed. According to Whitehead, they were pristine. No, Thelma Todd had been beaten and carried to the garage; she sure as hell hadn't *walked* there.

What if I'd been on Posetano on that particular December night instead of home in bed with Cissy? Could I have stopped Lucky's muscle man? Could I have saved this woman's life?

Probably not. I would have needed a gun, and I don't use guns. Dash Hammett might have been able to do something. He owns a .38 Police Positive, but he doesn't carry it unless he has a rea-son. I chuckled; Gardner could have used his bow and arrow on the guy—but then again you don't do much hunting at night on Posetano Road.

When I got back into my Duesenberg and drove down to the highway an orange glow filled the eastern edge of the sky. This trip to the murder site had inspired me. I was sure I could find a way to put Todd's case into a novelette for Joe Shaw. Every real-life murder is grist for a writer's creative mill. That's how we work. From a cold garage above the Pacific to the pulp pages of *Black Mask.*

Sorry about that, Thelma.

When I walked into our rented house in Culver City, my wife was seated on the living room sofa in a quilted pink satin robe, perusing Shakespeare. She looked up from the book, smiling.

4

"I was reading *Hamlet* again," she said. "The dead have so *much* to tell us, Raymio, yet cannot."

"The speech from the ghost of Hamlet's father . . . Is that what you're talking about?"

"Yes." She looked down at her book. "Where he says, 'I am forbid to tell the secrets of my prison-house. I could a tale unfold whose lightest word would harrow up thy soul, freeze thy young blood, make thy two eyes, like stars, start from their spheres. . . .'"

"I can think of a ghost or two I'd like to interview."

"Why are people afraid of them? I'd be delighted to meet one."

I smiled at her. Her face was lightly rouged but the paleness of her porcelain skin shone through the makeup, betraying her frailty. Cissy's mind had always been much stronger than her body, although she'd been quite striking in her youth. Several noted artists had painted her, and we kept an oil portrait of Cissy at twenty, bare-shouldered and regal, framed above the mantel. In the painting, her skin has an inner radiance, a glowing translucence like the finest bone china. To me, that beauty had never faded.

"The phone's been ringing," she told me. "I just wasn't up to answering it. I so dislike talking to salespeople."

"It might have been important."

"If it was, they'll phone back." She sighed. "Seems that someone is always trying to sell us life insurance."

"That's the Depression," I said. "People can't find any other job, so they begin calling other people, working on commission for some insurance company, trying to sell enough to eke out a living."

"I'm glad you don't have to do anything like that, Raymio."

I shook my head. "God knows I don't make a living from writing. If it wasn't for our oil stock—"

5

"Oh, don't let's talk about money." She stood up, hugging the book of plays to her chest. "Shakespeare was such a resourceful man. I'm sure he would have done well in the Depression."

"Sure. He could have written soap commercials."

"Please don't answer me with a wisecrack, darling." She walked over to kiss me lightly on the cheek. "I'm going to lie down for a while. I feel a bit weakish."

I nodded. Cissy spent a great part of each day lying down. The comfortable darkness of our bedroom seemed to satisfy a need in her. She was like a rare hothouse flower that can't be exposed to raw sunlight. When we go out together, for an occasional dinner or concert, it's nearly always at night. She prefers a life in shadow.

This is fine with me, since I'm very grateful to have her. She is my companion, my counselor, my great love. We care for one another deeply and completely, and that's everything. I can't imagine life without her.

As Cissy walked from the room she left behind the faint scent of jasmine. Her favorite perfume. For more than twenty years now the scent of jasmine has always reminded me of Cissy.

I sat down in the burgundy leather armchair in front of the chessboard and picked up a knight. The ivory chesspiece was cool against my fingers. I wondered anew how Cissy could put up with me.

In many ways, I'm a neurotic character. Freud would shake his head over me. Yet almost every writer I've known is neurotic. Writing is not an emotionally healthy occupation. This is particularly true if one writes pulp fiction. At least, that's what Cissy believes. She's waiting for me to write a "socially significant" novel. About my childhood or my life in England. Or about my years in the oil business. I promise her that I'll get around to it, but we both know I probably won't. I happen to take a perverse pleasure in writing about blondes and guns and gangsters, although, as Cissy keeps telling me, it's a creative dead end.

I hope she's wrong. When I finally get around to novels I'd like to do something special with crime fiction, maybe move it up a notch or two toward that rarified area known as "literature." Hammett says he felt the same way once, and that he tried with *The Maltese Falcon* and almost brought it off with *The Glass Key*, but failed. He says it can't be done, and that's why he gave up crime novels. He calls *The Thin Man* "the last of the damn things."

In my opinion, he gave up too soon. His best stuff held the promise of greatness, but he never made that final artistic jump over the line. He says he's working on another novel, with no crime or murder in it, a novel that will win him the kind of critical acclaim he never got as a crime writer. But where are the pages? I think he's kidding himself. He should never have turned his back on what he did best. I think I have a chance to prove the literary potential of crime fiction, but I still have a lot to learn before I try my first novel.

I've thought a lot about what should go into it. It will be about crime, most certainly, and about a man of honor who combats it, a private detective much like the ones I've been writing about for *Black Mask*. I'll probably call him Mallory. Suggesting knighthood and honor. Or maybe that's too damn obvious. I'm a hopeless romantic at heart; I have to keep reining myself back or I'll gallop off into pathos and sentimentality. At least Hammett was never sentimental. That was one of his strengths.

The phone rang and I picked up the receiver. "Yes?"

"Is this the residence of Raymond Chandler?" The voice was male, hard-edged.

"Yes, I'm Chandler."

"I need to talk to your wife."

"She's not available right now," I said. "Who are you and what do you want?"

"My name's Harker. I'm a lieutenant with Central Homicide. We need to have Mrs. Chandler come down to the morgue to identify a body. Apparently, the gent knew her."

"A dead man?"

"He was the last time I had a gander at him," said Harker. When I didn't respond he cleared his throat uneasily, aware that his cop's humor wasn't playing. "Could you put Mrs. Chandler on the phone?" It was more of an order than a request.

"I told you, my wife is not available. She's resting." I hesitated. "Whose body is it?"

"Wallet identification lists him as Julian Pascal. Had a letter in his pocket addressed to your wife . . . thanking her for a music book she sent him for his birthday."

"My God!" I breathed. "Julian!" I was stunned. "Where did . . . I mean, how did he . . ."

"Caretaker found him in a Chinese cemetery in the Boyle Heights area of East Los Angeles," said Harker. "Bullet in the left temple. One shot. Obviously self-inflicted. Gun still in his hand." Harker's voice assumed a sharper edge. "Just exactly what *was* his relationship to your wife?"

"Julian was her former husband," I said slowly, still in shock over what I was hearing. I drew in a long breath. "Listen, Lieutenant, I can make the identification. Julian and I were close friends. I can come down there."

"That'll be dandy," said Harker. "You know where the morgue is?"

"I know."

"Come right away. I'll wait for you. Ask for me when you get there."

"I'll do that."

"Okay," he said, hanging up.

I stood with the phone in my hand, feeling numb. This didn't make any sense. What would drive Julian to kill himself? And why did he end his life in, of all places, a Chinese cemetery in East Los Angeles?

I went into the bedroom to tell Cissy, but she was asleep. I decided not to wake her. I needed to confirm the truth of Harker's words.

I put on my coat and headed for the Duesenberg.

On the way downtown I had a lot of time to think about Julian Pascal.

We first met at the Los Angeles home of a mutual friend, Warren Lloyd. That was in 1913. Southern California was a strange new country to me, since I'd spent my formative years in Europe.

Not that I'm British by birth. Actually, I was born in Chicago, but I didn't stay there long. My parents divorced when I was seven and, after the breakup of their marriage, I was never to see my father again. The man was a swine, a violent drunk. It was clear that he didn't give a bloody damn about me. Still, as a child I felt abandoned. My mother was Irish, and she was a wonderful, open-hearted soul who loved me without reservation. We were always extremely close, especially so after my father left.

She took me to England with her after the divorce. We lived with her family, who were rather well fixed financially, and I attended Dulwich Preparatory School. In American terms, a private secondary school for upper-middle-class boys. A very good institution with exceptionally high standards. Dulwich gave me a solid classical education—as well as a grounding in rugby and cricket. After more schooling in France and Germany I decided I wanted to become a writer. This led to my working as a freelance journalist in London for *The Academy*, *The Westminster Gazette*, and *The Spectator*.

The fact that I am a fiction writer today, however modest my success, is something of a miracle. My early essays and poems demonstrated a lamentable lack of originality. They were precious and mannered, written in a vein of High Romance. I was an intolerably arrogant young twerp who fancied himself a gifted intellectual. Fortunately no one else shared this misguided view. With encouragement and hard work I might ultimately have achieved the status of a second-rate poet and third-rate essayist. It was a blessing that I received no such encouragement.

I became desperate to escape England, associating it with personal failure. Still in my early twenties, I felt I had to make a new beginning, and I decided to abandon the idea of writing and head back to the States. I managed to borrow enough money to ship out for America in 1912. On a steamer into New York I was befriended by the Warren Lloyds, who were active in California's prosperous oil industry.

Lloyd had earned a Ph.D. in philosophy at Yale and his wife, Alma, was a singer and sculptor. Intellectually, we shared immediate common ground. I mentioned that I had been thinking about a trip to California, and they invited me to visit them when I got to Los Angeles. Lloyd promised to help me find work there.

It took me a while to reach the West Coast, after stopovers in St. Louis and Omaha, but by 1913 I was firmly situated in the City of Angels. I had an impecabbly tailored London-cut wool suit, an upper-crust English accent you could cut with an ax, and a healthy contempt for the natives. I never quite accepted the fact that I was one of them.

True to his word, Warren Lloyd got me a job. As a bookkeeper. I became part of a group of artists, writers, and musicians who gathered socially each weekend at the Lloyds' big home on South Bonnie Brae Street. Which is where I met Julian Pascal.

We shared a British background, since Julian had once served as a professor at the Guildhall School of Music in London. But the damp weather there affected his lungs and he moved to Southern California for health reasons. He had been flourishing here as a well-respected pianist and composer, not only as part of the local arts establishment, but in the moving picture business as well.

Physically, Pascal was frail and round-shouldered, with the large, sad eyes of a depressed spaniel and a soft, whispery voice. His tweed suits were baggy but stylish, and he often wore a plaid cap to hide his thinning hairline. He had flawless manners and was damn good at chess, which I particularly appreciated. But Julian was much more than a gentleman in the English sense. In so many ways, he was one of the finest human beings I had ever known.

But as much as I liked him, his wife interested me a lot more. I remember first seeing her at the piano, wearing a flowing rose-colored gown that accented her strawberry blonde hair, playing Chopin's stirring Polonaise in A-flat Major, her long, delicate fingers drifting expertly over the keys, her head moving gracefully with the powerful rhythm of the music. I was mesmerized.

Pearl was her first name, but everyone called her Cissy. Later that night, when we had a chance to talk, I was struck by her intelligence and cool wit, which was mixed with a chic, regal sophistication that appealed to the snobbish side of my personality. Of course, with her luminous skin and arresting dark brown eyes, she was a genuine beauty. I was mildly shocked and erotically titillated to learn she had once modeled in the nude for a fashion photographer.

Almost instantly, I fell in love with Cissy Pascal, and she gave me reason to believe that she found me equally fascinating. But she also made it plain that she loved her husband and would remain faithful to him—which meant that we were forced to substitute friendship for love. I liked Julian and decided to make the best of things.

11

At about this time Mother came over from London to live with me. I had settled into the life of a working Californian when the Great War came along. I prefer not to detail my part in this bloody conflict. Suffice to say, I enlisted in the Canadian army in the summer of 1917, saw action, and was honorably discharged in 1919.

I returned to Los Angeles—and to Cissy.

We were closer than ever, having exchanged many passionate love letters during the war, and she finally asked Julian for a divorce. It was granted in 1920. Surprisingly, my friendly relationship with Pascal remained intact. I admired his ability to accept a very difficult situation without rancor or bitterness. In truth, Cissy never stopped loving him; it was simply, as she confessed in her forthright way, that she loved me *more*. If I hadn't come along, they would likely never have parted.

Mother's illness prevented a quick marriage. I felt that I owed it to my mother to stay with her to the end. In 1924 she died of cancer and Cissy and I were married that February. The fact that my wife is eighteen years my senior seemed to raise a few eyebrows in others, but the age difference has never bothered either of us in the least. Love is ageless, and since our wedding I have always considered myself to be among the most fortunate of men.

Julian's work gradually took him out of our lives. After sound pictures came in, he used his Hollywood connections to obtain employment in the entertainment industry, composing music for a wide variety of films, and though Cissy and I didn't see much of him, we kept in touch. Cissy always remembered his birthday and would send him a carefully considered present, which he would unfailingly acknowledge with a gracious and affectionate note. This year it had been a leather-bound, turn-of-the-century English volume on musical development from ancient Egyptian times until the ascent of Constantine—which explained the letter found on his body.

It was painful to think of this talented, caring man as a "body." What had led him to suicide? The last time we had talked, some four months ago, he assured us that his health had stabilized, that he was working on a new picture, and that he looked forward to beating me at chess on his next visit to our home.

He never made it.

Instead, I was visiting *him*.

At the city morgue.

TWO

I parked in the lot behind the County Building and walked down a musty hallway to the main lobby. The morgue was at the end of another long hallway, no less musty, ending at a pair of double swing doors set into a veined marble facade. Nearby, another door of pebbled glass took me into a cramped office containing a desk mounded with stacked paperwork, three straight-back wooden chairs, several battered green filing cabinets, and a framed photo of FDR. He looked very content, considering he was in the city morgue, with his cigarette holder tilted at a jaunty angle, a merry twinkle in his eyes. Maybe he was thinking about the next election.

A horse-faced attendant in soiled white coveralls walked in just after I did. I asked to see Lieutenant Harker.

"Who might you be?" His eyes were slumberous, heavy-lidded.

"I might be the man Harker's waiting for."

"That's no answer," he said. "I need a name."

"Raymond Chandler."

"Wait here."

He moved through a rear door and returned a few seconds

later, accompanied by a tall bruiser in a brown gabardine suit that he was a size too big for. He had a bulldog jaw and a high shelf of brow above hard brown eyes the color of muddy water. Harker.

When we shook hands he showed me some teeth in a smile he obviously didn't use much, the kind of smile you take out of a drawer and dust off once a year.

"This way," he said, leading me through the rear office door and down a short corridor into a large, brightly lit central room smelling of disinfectant. The white-enamel paint bounced back the light, reflected on floor-to-ceiling rows of glass-windowed drawers set into the far wall. A special kind of filing cabinet.

"He's number fifteen," said Harker, sliding one of the long drawers out of the wall. The runners squeaked slightly, needing oil, and a misted vapor from the refrigerated pipes inside frosted the air.

The bulked figure on the cold steel slab was covered by a wrinkled gray sheet that badly needed bleach. Only the ankles and feet were visible. The big toe of the left foot had a tag looped around it bearing the number 15.

"Ready for a look?" asked Harker, holding the edge of the sheet.

I nodded, thinking: what if this isn't Julian? What if I look down into the face of a total stranger? Suddenly, I very much didn't want this to be Julian's body. Not him. No. Don't let it be Julian.

But it was.

"Well?" asked Harker in his hard-edged tone. "Is this the guy?"

"Yes," I said softly, staring at the dead face of my friend. "He's Julian Pascal."

I recalled Cissy's words regarding Shakespeare's shade, that "the dead have so *much* to tell us, yet cannot." Indeed, if he could speak, Julian would have much to tell us.

The bullet hole in his left temple had blackened at the edges. His eyes were closed. The lids were dark and sunken and his gray, lifeless skin was stretched tightly over the prominent bones of his face. He looked like an old man.

And he smelled of death.

"Christ!" I muttered, turning away as Harker slid the drawer back into its wall slot.

At least Cissy didn't have to see this, I thought. It would be difficult enough for her to accept Julian's death. I dreaded having to tell her.

In the office, the horse-faced morgue attendant was reading a science-fiction pulp. A drooling Thing from another planet, shaped like a tomato plant with three heads, was carrying off an exceptionally well-endowed young lady in a wispy pink space suit.

"Breeze!" snapped Harker.

Pulp in hand, Horseface shuffled from the room.

The lieutenant took a stubbed pencil from the desk and flipped open a pocket notepad. "Some questions," he said, motioning me toward one of the straight-back chairs.

I sat down.

He asked me about Julian. About who he was and who were his next of kin and what he did for a living and how long I'd known him and when my wife had seen him last and why did they get divorced and were there bad feelings between them and why, in my opinion, he'd committed suicide.

"Maybe he didn't," I found myself saying.

"Huh?"

"Maybe somebody put the gun to his head and pulled the trigger, then placed it in his hand."

"That's nuts," growled Harker.

Now my voice held an edge of its own. "Julian had no reason

to kill himself. He wasn't sick. He wasn't depressed. He had steady work and all the money he needed. Suicide doesn't wash."

"Dammit, you don't know what was in this guy's mind," argued Harker. "People kill themselves for a lot of reasons."

I shook my head. "Not him. Not Julian."

"Baloney!" snapped Harker. He picked up a typed sheet of paper from the desk. "This is a release form—to prove somebody showed to identify the body. Just sign it and you're free to go."

"Then you won't even *consider* the possibility that this could be murder?"

"You got it, mister. The guy stiffed himself, pure and simple. And that's the way it plays."

Shades of Thelma Todd.

I didn't say anything else to him.

I signed the paper and walked out of the building.

Cissy was still in our bedroom when I returned to the house, but she was awake, sitting with her back propped against two ruffled pillows, her eyes closed, listening to Duke Ellington's orchestra on the table radio.

Taki, our ink-black Persian, was sleeping at the foot of the bed, tucked into a dark ball of cat fur on the checked coverlet. I scratched her behind the ears, and the tip of her tail twitched languidly, to let me know she appreciated the scratching. But her eyes remained squeezed shut and she paid me no further notice. Snoozing was her primary job at the moment, and she didn't want to be disturbed. She'd be active enough later when she got hungry.

I started to say something to Cissy, but she raised a hand to silence me. She wanted to hear Ellington finish.

"What a marvelous talent," she said, after the number was

over. "His music is so *pure*. He brings a whole new perspective to jazz."

I walked over to the bedside table and switched off the radio. She looked startled.

"I thought you *liked* Duke Ellington."

"We need to talk."

I sat down on the side of the bed next to her and took her hand. She read the darkness in my face.

"There's something terribly wrong, isn't there? Tell me what's wrong."

"It's Julian," I said.

"Has he been in an accident? Is he injured?"

"He's dead."

The words were heavy stones, striking her. Cissy's head fell back against the pillows and her eyes were suddenly tearful. For a long moment there was a strained silence between us.

Then she said, in a pained whisper: "Oh, Raymio. I loved him *so* much!"

I gripped her hand. "He was a good man. This should never have happened."

"I must know everything," she said. "Tell me."

I did, right through the morgue scene and my argument with Harker. "They're convinced it was suicide."

"Nonsense!" she said tightly, leaning forward. "Julian would never do away with himself. Never!" She raised her head defiantly. The tears were gone and her brown eyes flashed with anger. "You must find out what really happened."

"I'm not a cop," I said. "What can I do?"

"You can do whatever it takes to uncover the truth."

"I suppose I could talk to the man at the cemetery, the caretaker who found Julian."

"Yes, that's it! Talk to him. It's a place to start."

Then, abruptly, the strength seemed to leave her, and she

18

slumped back against the pillows. "Oh, Julian . . . dear, *dear* Julian." And she closed her eyes.

I walked from our bedroom to the phone in the living room, dialed Central Homicide, and asked for Harker.

"Sorry, but the lieutenant's out," said the young male voice on the other end of the line. "I work with him. I'm Detective Cole. Can I be of help?"

"I hope so." I explained the situation to him, asking for the cemetery's address.

"It's over in Boyle Heights," he told me. "You go straight down First Street. About three miles past the big bridge over the L.A. River. Intersection of First and Eastern."

"Does the caretaker live on the grounds?"

"Yeah. In a shack at the rear. But going over there won't do you any good."

"Why not? Isn't he willing to talk?"

"Sure, he's willing," said Cole. "Talks like a goddam magpie. But you won't be able to understand a word the old gink says."

"How come?"

"He only speaks Cantonese. Didn't Harker tell you it was a *Chinese* cemetery?"

I hesitated for a moment, thinking. "That's no problem. I'll take along a friend who speaks the language."

"You know somebody who speaks Cantonese?" he asked, skepticism in his tone.

"A fellow writer," I said. "His name is Erle Stanley Gardner."

He calls himself "the fiction factory." Words spill out of him like water over a dam. Last year alone, he had three serials, eighteen novelettes, and four new books published, including two Perry Mason novels. And he isn't selling only to the rough-paper magazines these days. In '35, in addition to his output for the pulps, Erle was printed in *Liberty, This Week,* and *Field and*

Stream. His books are moving steadily up the sales chart and the Warner boys continue to pump out new Mason pictures.

While I have always admired Erle's remarkable talent for fast production, he's not in the same league with Hammett or a dozen other crime writers I could name. Gardner is a genius at meeting the needs of the popular market, but his work lacks creative depth—the kind of quality you find in a book such as *The Maltese Falcon.* Then again, he makes no pretense at greatness; he's happy as a clam just racking out his action-packed books and stories, and I suspect he'll go on pleasing the reading public for as long as he chooses to keep writing. But with Erle, you never know. He just might hop in his truck, drive off into the wilds, and never produce another word. He loves exploring new places.

We trust each other. Our friendship has been tested under fire. Last year, Erle and I shared a wild adventure with Dashiell Hammett—chasing down a missing jeweled skull—which is when I happened to find out that Gardner speaks Cantonese. He and Dash had followed up a lead in San Francisco's Chinatown. Hammett couldn't speak the language, but Erle had no trouble with it. Later, when I asked him where he'd learned Cantonese, he told me that he had represented the Chinese community in various court actions during his days as a lawyer in Oxnard, California.

Now I needed Gardner's expertise, and phoned him at his home in the Hollywood hills.

Tomas, his Filipino houseboy, told me that "Mister Erle" was working in his trailer behind the garage. I dialed him there, and he picked up on the first ring.

"Gardner," he said.

"Hi, chum, it's Ray."

"Hey, there!" He seemed happy to hear my voice.

"Hope I didn't interrupt the latest Mason saga."

"No, no . . . I'm doing a new Win Layton."

"Is that a pen name or a character?"

"Character. I call her 'the Girl Reporter.' My agent thinks he can sell her to *This Week*. Big bucks."

"Well, good luck," I said.

"You sound kind of odd. Something wrong?"

I told him about Julian, where his body was found, and that I needed Erle to go with me to interview the Chinese caretaker.

"Glad to help," he said. "When do you plan to talk to the guy?"

"Right away. Could I pick you up in about forty minutes?"

"Jake with me. I could use a break. I'll be waiting in front of the house." A pause. "How did Cissy take the news?"

"First she cried. Then she got mad. She doesn't believe it was suicide, and neither do I. I'm supposed to find out what actually happened."

"Think you can?"

"It's possible. At least, I'm going to try. I'm damn well going to try."

Gardner was waiting on the walk fronting his house under the shade of a tall pepper tree when I drove up to him in the Duesenberg. He was wearing white golf slacks, soft-soled white shoes, and a white blazer with his initials, ESG, stitched into the left pocket.

"You must get a lousy miles-to-the-gallon average in this tub," he said, settling into the passenger side.

"It's not a tub," I snapped back. "It's one of the finest automobiles in the world."

"I'm well aware of how fine it is. In fact, you've told me more about the Duesenberg than I ever cared to know. But I'm talking miles to the gallon."

"So who cares?" I said, heading down La Brea toward Wilshire. Traffic was light and we were sailing along. "How many miles you get to the gallon is not relevant when you drive a masterpiece. Did Shakespeare worry about how much paper it took to write *Hamlet?* Did Michelangelo worry about how much paint he used on the ceiling of the Sistine Chapel?"

"I hate it when you go classical on me."

And we exchanged grins. Full-faced, chunky, with twinkling eyes behind round, steel-rimmed glasses, Erle reminded me of an out-of-season Santa. Only the white beard was missing.

We began talking about Julian.

"And you're *convinced* it's murder?"

I nodded. "Absolutely. At first, when they told me it was suicide, I tried to make some sense of it. The more I thought about Julian killing himself, the crazier it seemed."

"I never knew him," said Gardner. "But I know how much he meant to you and Cissy."

We drove in silence for a while. Then I said, "I remember, right after the divorce, we talked about suicide and Julian claimed that a man would have to be an utter fool to end his own life."

"Maybe," said Erle. "Yet . . . if you're depressed over money . . . women . . . a terminal illness . . . suicide might seem the one logical out. It would solve all your problems."

"Julian *had* no problems," I replied, easing around a slow-moving Bennett Dairies milk truck. "He was one of the most deeply contented individuals I've ever known. And totally pragmatic. He accepted whatever life handed him. Even when Cissy asked him for the divorce so she could marry me he took it right in stride. He still loved her, but he didn't stand in her way. Julian never let emotion dictate his actions—and suicide is a very emotional act."

"Amen," nodded Gardner.

I turned left from La Brea and drove Wilshire all the way

downtown. Then I took Main to First Street, turned right, and kept on First, crossing the long bridge that separates the downtown area from East Los Angeles. We passed over the rail tracks and the L.A. River, swollen from recent storms, and continued east past rows of big Victorian houses and red-brick apartment buildings. Boyle Heights was slowly losing its shine; it had seen better days, but it was still hanging in there.

As we approached Eastern Avenue the cemetery was in plain sight to our right, taking up a couple of city blocks, surrounded by a ten-foot-high spike-tipped iron picket fence. The words *Chinese Cemetery* in scrolled letters—repeated, no doubt, in the black-metaled Chinese characters underneath—formed an arch above the wide iron gate.

The sky seemed suddenly darker.

We had reached Julian's death site.

THREE

We rolled slowly uphill along a narrow gravel road, past rows of marble grave markers. I parked at the edge of a circular driveway, facing a red concrete platform that overlooked the cemetery grounds. We got out of the Duesenberg and walked over to the platform. What appeared to be a small stone altar was centered on it, flanked by a pair of large, white-painted pagoda-shaped structures with edged brick chimneys. A rusted iron door, held shut by a metal latch, was set into each of them.

On the altar, in a shallow dirt-filled concrete depression, were several bamboo sticks tied with yellow ribbons, some old orange peels, wilted flowers, and the remnants of several red firecrackers. To either side of the altar were white plaster incense holders a foot high.

"What's all this?" I asked Gardner.

"Part of Qing Ming. It was celebrated here late last month."

"Qing Ming?"

"Means All Souls' Day," Erle stated. "A time to honor the dead. Big event for the Chinese." He pointed to the altar. "They bring food—oranges are traditional—and flowers here for their ancestors, then light firecrackers to frighten off evil spirits.

There was a cemetery like this when I was in Oxnard, only it was smaller."

"What about the bamboo sticks with the ribbons?"

"More protection. Helps keep away wandering spirits who might otherwise despoil the graves. The Chinese worry a lot about spirits."

I indicated the two pagoda-shaped white structures. "And these?"

"Incinerators," replied Erle, lifting the latch and opening one of the iron doors. "Have a look."

I leaned down to peer inside. Ashes. Lots of ashes. And some sheets of half-burned paper. I pulled out a scrap, edged in silver foil.

"Mock money," said Gardner. "Joss paper, imprinted with silver. For the dead."

"I don't get it."

"The whole idea is to provide the 'celestial ones'—their deceased ancestors—with all the good stuff they might need in the afterlife. So they create paper models of desirable objects and burn them here. The essence of each object is released in the smoke, which then wafts up to where the celestial ones live."

"Including fake money?"

"You bet. Money is a primary item. Also models of houses, cars, furniture . . . even pots and pans."

I nodded. "That's like the early Egyptian burial customs—when they put all the king's treasures in the tomb with him, to help him enjoy his journey to the afterlife."

"Along the same lines," agreed Erle. "In ancient times the Chinese actually burned the real goods. Then it was clay models. Now, it's paper. But it all amounts to the same thing, providing the dead with what it's figured they'll need."

"Is there a payoff?"

"Definitely," Gardner said. "The shades of the departed report the generosity of their descendants to the high powers so these big-time supernatural deities will be inclined to bestow earthly rewards."

"And all this happens every year?"

"Yep. In late March or early April. They also do a kind of spring cleaning of the graves. You know, getting rid of the weeds, polishing the marble, putting down flowers and food."

We left the platform to inspect some of the grave sites. I checked names carved into the headstones: Quon Shoong . . . Woo May Hing . . . Wong Sai Gam . . . Tuey Kock Num . . .

There were shriveled apples and oranges at the foot of several markers, as well as red candles that had melted to wax stubs. Beyond the usual California palms, I noted an inordinate number of tall willow trees shading the graves. I asked Gardner about them.

"Willow trees are believed to possess a miraculous power over demons," Erle told me.

I dusted some grave dirt off my trousers. "I've seen enough. Let's find the caretaker."

He lived exactly where Detective Cole had said he lived: in a small shack at the far uphill end of the cemetery, about a hundred feet behind the altar and furnaces. As we approached his place, I noticed that the head of a tortoise protruded from a shelf above the door. When I pointed it out to Erle, he had an explanation.

"It's there to insure long life. Cut the head off a tortoise, mount it above your door, and you'll live to a ripe old age."

"I doubt that the tortoise sees it that way," I said.

We were within fifty feet of the shack when the door popped open and the caretaker emerged, wearing light blue overalls and strap sandals, and looking agitated. Jabbering Chinese in a rapid flow, he trotted up to us, frantically pointing toward my Duesenberg.

"He's upset," Gardner reported.

"I can see that," I said. "But over what?"

"Your back wheels are on the grave of one of his honored ancestors. Also, he says your car is too big. Big cars in his cemetery make him nervous."

"Tell him I'll move it," I said.

I did that, parking in the center of the gravel driveway. Even if I blocked another vehicle, at least my wheels were off his sacred ancestor.

When I got back to Gardner and the caretaker they were standing on the red platform, exchanging Cantonese. The caretaker had grown a wispy beard that formed a gray mist over his chin; his thin lips quivered with the flow of words, and the hairs on his beard wagged up and down as he talked. He was very intense, gesturing vigorously to emphasize each statement. Now he gestured toward a spot directly in front of the altar.

"This is where he found the body," said Gardner.

Another rapid exchange of Cantonese.

"He says he discovered Pascal early this morning, that he'd never seen him before, and that he was very shocked to find a ghost in his cemetery."

"A *ghost?*"

"That's Chinese for a white man."

"Did he see anyone else on the grounds?"

"Nope."

"Did he hear the shot?"

"No, he was sleeping. But he's absolutely sure it's suicide."

That surprised me. "How can he be sure?"

More singsong Cantonese.

"Apparently Pascal knew quite a lot about Chinese culture."

"Why do you say that? He certainly never mentioned the subject to Cissy or me."

"From what the caretaker says, Pascal believed in Feng Shui."

"Never heard of it."

"It's an ancient Chinese philosophical study which maintains that the positioning and placement of any object exerts a profound influence on our lives."

The caretaker was peering at me intently as Erle continued his translation. I grinned at him, but there was no change of expression on his solemn face. I guess he didn't care much for ghosts.

"According to Jiong Yan—that's his name, by the way—anyhow, according to Yan, the body was positioned 'most auspiciously.' "

"Auspiciously? How in the devil can a body be positioned 'auspiciously'?"

"Pascal was in a half-sitting position, facing downhill, and his body was supported by the incense burner on the right. Thus, his back was against the dragon."

"What dragon?"

"It's the hill we're on. This is the dragon. All part of the Chinese Feng Shui system."

"Go on," I nodded.

"Yan says the ghost made sure that his body was facing downhill, toward the watercourse."

"There's no water around here."

Gardner pointed to a narrow, adobe brick trench running through the grounds from east to west.

"It's dry now," he declared, "but it fills whenever there's a heavy rain."

"So all this mystical stuff you're telling me about is what makes the caretaker sure it was suicide?"

"Exactly. To Yan, it's obvious."

I shook my head. "It could be sheer coincidence. There's nothing here to convince me that any of this was deliberate on Julian's part."

Gardner conveyed my skepticism to Jiong Yan, who bowed to

us, excused himself in a spatter of Cantonese, and trotted uphill toward his shack.

"Where's he going?"

"He says he needs to show us something."

When the caretaker returned he was carrying an oriental red-and-gold-framed vanity mirror which was mounted on what looked like a carved teakwood base. He pointed to the concrete platform, then to the mirror, talking a mile a minute.

Gardner listened, nodding. "Yan found this next to the body. Mirrors hold a special significance to the Chinese."

"I still don't—"

"He says the mirror was exactly positioned to deflect Pascal's departing spirit. But unfortunately its position also placed Yan in great danger. Seems the thing was angled toward Yan's living quarters, meaning that any stray spirits in the vicinity would be directed toward him. That's why he removed it."

"And you actually believe that Julian was aware of all this weird stuff?"

Gardner frowned at me. "Weird to you, Ray, but not to anyone who understands Chinese religion. I happen to know precisely what Jiong Yan is talking about, and he's right. Pascal may not have been Chinese, but he obviously followed their culture, at least in the manner of his death. Everything points to a ritual suicide."

"Not to me it doesn't. Did Yan tell all this to the cops?"

Gardner asked the caretaker what he had told the police when they'd interviewed him.

"He just showed them where he'd found the body," Erle said, "but he didn't mention the mirror or the other stuff. Says he didn't like answering their questions. He's willing to trust me because I speak his language."

"Let's go," I said. "I've had enough of this."

Erle bowed, thanked Jiong Yan profusely, and we left the cemetery. The caretaker looked relieved as we drove away.

The ghosts had departed.

After dropping off Gardner at his house I returned home. It was now late afternoon and the sun was riding down the western edge of the sky. My long shadow unwound ahead of me as I crossed our lawn to key open the front door.

Taki was waiting. She gave me a dirty look and turned her back on me, heading for the kitchen. It was past time for her saucer of milk—which she enjoys promptly at three each day—and I'd trifled with her schedule.

I'll admit that Taki is spoiled. Cissy and I dote on her. I suppose you could call her the child we never had. It's been my observation that childless couples seem to be a lot closer, emotionally, to their pets.

Taki won't tolerate another animal in the house. She has her own strong ideas about creatures. People are good to rub against and they are also good for getting scratched behind the ears. Fish are boring. A butterfly is fun to chase, but too erratic. Yard lizards are interesting because they are capable of discarding their tails in times of stress.

Taki is not at all sadistic, and she doesn't kill things. However, like all cats, she's a hunter. At various times she has trotted proudly into the kitchen with a squirming creature in her mouth, anxious to impress us with her hunting prowess. Once her trophy was a small gray mouse, who looked terrified. Then she carried in a baby garden snake. Another time it was a blue parakeet. Each was unharmed. When we took them back outside, Taki was annoyed. She'd brought them in for *us*, after all.

She's three years old. We've had her since I started writing for the *Mask* in 1933. At night, she sleeps at the foot of our bed.

Lately, she's taken to snoring; when this bothers me, I just give her a nudge with my toe and she stops.

I've always been partial to cats over dogs. Personal preference. For one thing, cats are not sentimental and they never slobber. Most dogs are too frantic. I appreciate the poise and tranquil manner of a cat; they have an immense sense of personal dignity. And they don't bark. Taki *does* purr quite loudly when she's content—a buzzing sound, like a tiny outboard motor.

It's tough being egotistic around her. While I'm at the typewriter she sprawls across my desk, staring out of the window. When I finish a section on a new story I often read it aloud to her because I know she fancies herself a perceptive critic of my work. She'll talk to me about it for five minutes at a stretch, looking me straight in the eye. I'm sure it's excellent criticism that I could well profit by, but the fact is, I can't understand a word she says.

But she keeps trying.

I was washing out Taki's saucer when Cissy walked into the kitchen. She was in a gauzy, peach-colored lounging robe, and her eyes were red and swollen. She'd been crying a lot.

"Did Taki get her milk?"

"Every lick of it," I said, drying the saucer and putting it back on the cabinet shelf. "When she finished, she stuck her tail in the air and stalked out. She's sore at me for being late."

Cissy sat down at the kitchen table, looking drawn and weary. The shock of Julian's death had taken a lot out of her.

"The police phoned," she said. "They wanted to know the addresses of Julian's mother and sister in Connecticut. I gave them the information, including the phone number, but asked if I could have the chance to tell Ada and Helen first."

"Did you call?"

"Yes. Of course, they were extremely upset. And I lied. I told them the cause of death has yet to be determined. I just couldn't bear to . . ."

She lapsed into a pained silence, head down.

"What about funeral arrangements?"

"Ada asked me to take care of it. The family has no roots in Connecticut, they moved there just a few years ago, and she thinks it best if Julian is buried where he felt most at home— here in California."

"Are they coming out for the services?"

"No. Since she broke her hip last year, Ada hasn't left the house, and she's totally dependent on Helen for her care. So neither one of them can come." Cissy thought for a moment. "It's probably better that way. Going to the burial might kill Ada. Julian was always her favorite, you know."

Cissy looked up at me. "I also phoned Margaret in Toronto."

"How did she take the news?"

"Horribly. You know how much she cared about Julian . . . how she depended on him. She's canceling the rest of her concert tour and taking the train back to Los Angeles. She'll be here in time for the funeral. I invited her to stay with us, of course."

Among Julian Pascal's stellar qualities was his willingness to encourage and guide younger talent. He always had at least one or two protégés under his creative wing, and he had told us, three years before, that he considered Margaret Stetler the most gifted student he'd yet encountered. Julian felt that she deserved top international status—including guest appearances at Carnegie Hall—but, of course, he knew this wasn't likely. Negroes don't become concert pianists. Not in the United States of America, they don't.

He urged her to try building a reputation outside the country; perhaps it would eventually result in her being accepted on the concert stage here. Margaret took his advice.

She'd done sensationally well in Paris, where there is virtually no color bar in the upper cultural echelons. Her Paris contract had been extended several times. She'd also done well in Amsterdam, in Copenhagen and Stockholm, and in Brussels, Rome, Madrid, and Lisbon.

She'd capped off her European tour with another series of concerts in Paris, which confirmed her stellar status among the French. That led to successful performances in French-speaking Canada, then in Ottawa and Toronto.

All in all, she'd done far better than anyone had thought possible.

We're very fond of Margaret—a sweet, honest person whose wisdom far exceeds her years. She has always given Julian full credit for the success she's enjoyed; to her, he was the gentle and loving father she'd never had.

"My throat is so dry," Cissy told me. "I squeezed some oranges from the tree. Would you please get me a glass of juice? There's a pitcher of it in the icebox."

"I'll join you," I said, bringing out the pitcher and pouring two glasses. I sat down next to her at the kitchen table.

"Did you find out anything at the cemetery?" Cissy asked.

I filled her in on what Gardner and I had seen there, described the place where Julian's body had been discovered, and repeated everything that the caretaker had told us.

"A lot of nonsense!" declared Cissy, her eyes flashing.

"Maybe not. Erle claims that Jiong Yan is right, that Julian died as a ritual suicide."

"Did Yan tell the police that?"

"No," I said. "He doesn't trust them. And if they had all this extra evidence it would just help prove what they already believe."

I finished my juice, pushing the glass away from me, then rubbed my forehead, frowning.

"And what do you think now, Raymio?"

"I don't know *what* to think," I admitted. "Did Julian ever talk to you about any of this Chinese stuff?"

"No, never," she said. She pursed her lips. "But once he did have what one might term a Chinese experience. About seven years ago. He was just getting into sound films, and he worked on a picture that was supposed to be set in Hong Kong. Actually, of course, it was shot in Hollywood. I can't recall the title . . . something about a dragon."

"Yes, I remember now . . . *The Dragon's Daughter.*"

"Julian wrote the music for it."

I shrugged. "So what? He wrote the music for that historical film about Alexander the Great's invasion of India, too, but he sure didn't become a Hindu. I can't believe that his work on one low-budget Chinese quickie could explain what happened at that cemetery."

"It does seem improbable," Cissy agreed.

I stood up from the table. "I need Julian's address. Didn't he move in January?"

"Yes . . . to an apartment in Hollywood. He wanted to be closer to the studios." She looked intently at me. "Why do you need his address?"

"Because I'm going there to look the place over."

"The police told me that they had searched his apartment and found no evidence of foul play."

"That doesn't prove anything. They weren't *looking* for evidence. I want to see for myself."

"But how will you get in?"

"I'll handle it," I said. Then, softening my tone: "Please, Cissy . . ."

She sighed, obviously not happy with my plan. "Apartment 316 at the Humboldt Arms. On the corner of Hollywood and Highland."

*   *   *

I drove over there and parked a block down from the corner address. Since my Duesenberg is about as inconspicuous as a leprechaun at a Jewish wedding, I didn't want to attract undue attention.

A big red interurban streetcar rumbled along Hollywood Boulevard, jangling its warning bell as it crossed Highland. I walked past a sizable crowd in the forecourt of Sid Grauman's theater where some female star with big hips and a vacuous smile was standing in a patch of wet cement, leaving her footprints for posterity. Not that posterity gave a damn.

The Humboldt Arms was a respectable-looking three-story buff-brick apartment building with a fieldstone wall separating it from the street. I walked under a fringed canopy through polished brass swing doors into a wide lobby full of potted palms and stale afternoon air.

A raw-faced kid was holding down the reception desk. I swaggered up to him, flipped open my wallet for a split second, muttered "Police," and demanded the key to apartment 316. The kid had spiky red hair and an apologetic chin that disappeared into his collar. He didn't look too bright, which I was counting on, because if he asked for a close gander at my identification I was cooked. He hesitated, staring at me.

"Snap it up, sonny," I growled, shoving my right palm toward him. "Gimme!"

He blinked, took the proper key from a pegboard behind the desk, and handed it over. "I thought you people were through in there."

"Not quite," I snapped, crossing the sun-faded rose carpet to the elevator. I knew he was watching me, still uncertain. To back up my act, after pressing the "Up" button, I spat into a tall glazed sand jar by the elevator door. It was effective. Cops spit a lot.

Behind the swagger, I was nervous.

I didn't know what I'd find in apartment 316.

FOUR

After closing the door of Julian's apartment behind me I stood unmoving in the darkness, allowing my fast-beating heart to calm itself. Being here in his personal living quarters on the same day he died was traumatic for me. I had to fight the horrific feeling that his shade, like the ghost of Hamlet's father, haunted these silent rooms.

I switched on the lights, dispelling the shadows, and told myself I was an idiot for giving in to such melodramatic fancies. I thought of the scene in Hammett's *Dain Curse* when the protagonist, drugged with chloroform, becomes locked in a surreal struggle with a ghost, only to discover he's been fighting plumes of steam. I shook these images from my mind and looked over the apartment.

It was neatly furnished, mostly with things that I recognized from having known Julian for so many years: deep-cushioned, comfortable armchairs, a large mirror edged in blue glass over the mantel; and bright-hued, abstract paintings on the walls. A long, pale blue davenport, with fat throw pillows as white as an angel's wing, faced a glass-topped carved ebony-wood coffee table. And, of course, dominating the room was Julian's piano, a handsome Steinway, its richly polished mahogany gleaming in the glow of the lights.

I recalled how fascinated Julian had always been by the history of the instrument he loved, how he'd told us about Bartolomeo Cristofori, a Florentine harpsichord maker, who had fashioned a pioneer version of the piano in 1709 which he named *gravicembalo col piano e forte*. Julian was fond of pointing out that he followed in the grand tradition of Mozart and Haydn, who were the first major composers to write for the piano. I wondered what they'd think of Pascal's musical contributions to *The Dragon's Daughter*.

I picked up a *Saturday Evening Post* from the coffee table. Norman Rockwell had painted the cover for this issue, which featured an article on film music; Julian was probably mentioned in it, but I didn't bother to find out.

There was a small den, or working office, just off the main living room, with an antique blue-and-white Persian rug covering the hardwood floor. In one corner a black-leather easy chair had been placed next to a tall Philco radio in a walnut cabinet. A brass floor lamp with a faded yellow shade stood beside an oak writing desk. Scored pages from Julian's latest musical composition were strewn across the desk. An antique Dutch cigar box with brass hinges was filled with sharpened pencils; Julian had never smoked.

I investigated each drawer of the desk, sifting through a variety of papers and business correspondence, but found nothing related to Pascal's death. The lowest drawer on the right side held a fat bundle of Cissy's letters, many dating back to their courtship and marriage. I slipped them into my coat. With Julian gone, they belonged to Cissy now.

The den walls were crowded with photos of Julian posing next to various industry notables—shots of him on the set with Gable and Harlow and Crawford, plus a large photo, framed in silver, of Pascal at the piano during one of his New York concerts.

I turned my attention to a large open-shelved oak bookcase, scanning the titles for a possible clue to Julian's death.

And there it was—sandwiched between *The Encyclopedia of Classic Music, Fourth Edition*, and *History's Great Composers*—a book on Chinese culture. At least that's what it appeared to be from the interior woodcut illustrations. I couldn't tell from the text itself, which was entirely in Chinese. Julian's name was printed, in the characteristic royal blue ink he always used, on the front flyleaf.

I was stunned. Did he actually know how to read Chinese?

The important thing now was to find out exactly what this book contained.

"Well . . ." Erle said, riffling the pages, "this definitely deals with Chinese culture, but it's fairly specialized material; I can make out only a limited number of words."

"I thought you were the great Chinese expert," I said.

We were in his trailer which was, as usual, jammed floor to ceiling with sports paraphernalia, attesting to the fact that Erle Stanley Gardner was the ultimate outdoorsman.

The sky beyond the window was the color of charcoal; darkness had descended as I'd driven here.

Erle bristled at my words. "I'm no damned expert," he snapped. "Never claimed to be. Sure, I can *speak* Cantonese, but I can't read much of the language. I know maybe a thousand characters, tops. Not even enough to read a newspaper easily." He tapped a finger against the book. "But I can see that it's all here."

"What is?" I asked, afraid of the answer.

"The whole suicide situation," said Gardner. He turned to a fully illustrated section, matching words to pictures. "These drawings demonstrate how to position a mirror to deflect a departing spirit . . . exactly how to angle your body for a ritual death . . . all the Feng Shui stuff.''

"My God!" I breathed. "Then Julian really *did* kill himself."

Gardner nodded solemnly. "Sure looks that way."

I phoned Cissy from the trailer, telling her about the book I'd found, and what it meant.

"I know it's tough, but we'll just have to accept Julian's death as a suicide," I said.

"Why *should* we?" she flared back. "I feel certain Julian could not read Chinese. In fact, he felt guilt over never having mastered another language. Most classical musicians learn French, German, and Italian. Julian never did. He couldn't read Chinese any more than you can."

"But the book was in his library, and *his* name is written on the flyleaf in that royal blue ink he always used."

"That doesn't convince me it actually belonged to him," she declared. "And even if it did, think about those canopic jars your mother bought in the shop at the British Museum. They've got ancient Egyptian hieroglyphs painted on them, and they're on the shelf in our living room, but that doesn't mean that you or I can *read* the hieroglyphs."

"I see what you're saying," I said.

"Raymio, we have to keep looking for the truth in all this. We haven't found it yet."

"You're a stubborn soul," I said softly.

"No, I'm just a woman who loved Julian Pascal very deeply, and knew him better than anyone else ever could. And I tell you, Raymio, he did *not* commit suicide. Every atom of my being shouts out 'murder.' '' Her voice rang over the wire. "It was murder!"

At ten o'clock the next morning I was in L.A.'s Chinatown, talking to the proprietor of the China Book Company. Erle had pointed out that the end page of the book from Julian's apartment had carried a rubber-stamped impression, in Chinese, giving the name and location of the store from which the book had been purchased.

Mr. Chang, the owner, was a friendly, quick-smiling gentleman of advanced years who spoke broken English. I showed him the book, which he recognized, and a photo of Julian, which he didn't.

"Who bought the book?" I asked.

"White woman," he answered. "Most unusual. Sold book to white woman."

I asked him to describe her, but he couldn't. Perhaps he had forgotten, or perhaps to him all "ghosts" looked alike. I kept asking questions, and he kept shaking his head, smiling, and saying "no." He couldn't remember if the woman was young or old, short or tall, fat or thin, and he couldn't remember when the book had been sold.

Frustrated, I thanked him and left the store.

My trip downtown had proved nothing. Julian could have had a female friend pick up the book for him. Or it might have been a gift. Despite Cissy's conviction, *could* Julian have read the text? Had he become fascinated with Chinese rituals and customs?

At the moment, there was no way of knowing.

Fewer than a dozen people attended Julian's burial two days later. Cissy and I, Erle, Margaret, and a small group of industry people—none of whom I knew—were seated under a canvas canopy in a row of chairs a few feet from the raised coffin.

The depression we all felt was augmented by a hard-driving rain that drummed the coffin and streamed down the sides of the newly dug burial trench. Cissy had an arm around Margaret's shoulders as the Episcopal priest, in clerical collar and a long black slicker, quoted a Bible passage related to everlasting life.

White hair plastered to his skull, his glasses fogged and wet, he intoned the words in a voice that was barely audible above the drumming rain.

Margaret had slept fitfully the previous night on the train and looked exhausted. Her normally attractive face was drawn; her large brown eyes were haunted by grief, and her lips trembled as she fought for emotional control.

The minister asked if anyone "here assembled" would care to say a few words about the deceased. No one volunteered, so I stepped forward, not really prepared but determined to pay my old friend a final tribute.

The rain increased its intensity, slashing into the raw brown earth, cutting a dark wound in the spread of emerald grass surrounding the grave.

"Julian Pascal deserves to be remembered . . ." My voice faltered as I ran my gaze across the other mourners; Gardner nodded, encouraging me to continue. "He was, of course, a supremely gifted pianist and composer, dedicated to his craft and tireless in his pursuit of excellence. He was also a gracious, caring man who generously shared his time and talent with others in whom he believed." I was looking at Margaret; tears were flowing along her cheeks. "He was a loving man, loyal and unselfish and kind; he was a true friend, a superb human being, and we have all been blessed by having had him in our lives." Cissy began to cry openly.

I placed my right hand on the cold, wet wood of the coffin. The flowers banked over it had been flattened and battered by the rain, and their colors were now mixed and blended. My final words were from Shakespeare, dramatic but heartfelt: "Good night, sweet prince, and flights of angels sing thee to thy rest!"

As I resumed my seat, Cissy squeezed my hand, nodding through her tears. Margaret's head was down, her body shaken by sobs.

It was then that I noticed the tall, veiled figure of a woman standing a few hundred yards from our group, at the edge of the crushed-gravel cemetery road. A long white Cadillac limousine was parked just behind her, and when she saw me looking toward her, she turned away and entered the white car. I saw her gesture to the driver, and the limo motored off, quickly disappearing behind the silver curtain of rain.

At home the next morning I was back on "Goldfish," the novelette I was finishing for *Mask*, completing final revisions. Cissy had taken to her bed, still in shock over Julian, and I was working in the second bedroom, which had been converted into my office. Taki was curled up on my three-drawer green metal filing cabinet; I'd spread a thick yellow bath towel over the top for her and she was happily snoozing, one paw draped over her closed eyes to shut out the sunlight from the window.

"Goldfish" was almost done. The final page was completed inside my head and all I had to do was finish it on paper. I didn't have much left to tinker with, just this last page, but it had to be right. I'm hypercritical about my stuff; I never send out anything that isn't as perfect as I can make it. And I learn more with each story.

This one had a neat windup. My detective was after some stolen pearls, and I'd figured out a clever way to hide them. Earlier in the story I'd mentioned these big Moors, lazy, thick-bodied fish with telescope eyes. At the climax, my detective opens them up to find the missing pearls sewn into their bellies. I knew Joe Shaw would love the idea.

I'd just lifted one of the Moors from the tank (on paper, that is) when the phone rang. It was Hammett, calling from Global Studios. He'd returned the previous weekend from a film location in Arizona, was already on another picture, and wanted to see me.

"Sorry I couldn't make the funeral," he said. "I talked to Erle, and he told me all about your murder theory."

"It's Cissy's murder theory," I declared. "Did Gardner also tell you about the book I found?"

"Yeah, he did."

"Well, up to then, I couldn't accept the fact that Julian's death was a suicide. But now I do. I still don't know *why* he killed himself. There obviously had to be some kind of deep problem in his life that none of us knew about, but I think the evidence is strong enough to eliminate the idea of foul play. However, Cissy won't budge. To her, it's murder."

"Come over to Global and tell me about it. Erle didn't give me much on the phone. I'm curious."

"It's the Pinkerton in you," I said. "Always looking for a crime angle. Can't you ever give up being a sleuth?"

"Hey, pal, I gave that up fourteen years ago, remember?"

"Technically, you did. But based on what we went through last year, looking for that damned jeweled skull, I'd say you still get a big kick out of playing detective."

"I was just trying to help out Joe Shaw," he claimed. "Nothing more to it."

"Uh-huh."

"Get your butt over here and let's talk. I'm in bungalow eight. They handed me a crappy outline about a three-hundred-year-old vampire with an Oedipus complex, and I'm trying like the devil to keep from having to start scripting it. You'll provide a welcome diversion."

I told him okay, that I'd be there as soon as I wrapped up the climax to "Goldfish" for *Mask*, and that I intended to drop the manuscript into the mail on the way over.

"You're becoming Joe's star writer," Hammett said. "I hope he's paying you more than I got."

"I'm getting his top rate," I said, "but I'm still starving."

43

"That's because you're too damn slow!"

"I'm *meticulous*," I corrected. "Quality can't be rushed."

"I keep telling you, come work in pictures. These studio people love dumping money on writers."

"I'll leave the scripting to you," I said. "Right now I'm still learning how to turn out decent prose."

Hammett had been assigned one of the new writers' bungalows on the corner of the Global lot, just behind a row of tall, concrete-walled soundstages. A knight in full armor, carrying a long wooden sword, clanked past me. A trio of giggly dancing girls in flouncy red skirts entered the nearest soundstage just behind the knight, and they were followed by a bored-looking propman lugging a rubber cactus.

Hammett's place was impressive. It had its own bathroom and kitchenette, and the main workroom contained a king-sized couch, glass-topped desk, six comfortable chairs, and a varnished walnut conference table. Papers and scripts were stacked on the desk next to Hammett's typewriter.

"How was Yuma?" I asked after we'd shaken hands.

"It was hell," said Hammett. "Hundred ten in the shade, when you could find some, with the heat coming at you from the sky *and* the sand. And speaking of heat, I could use a cold drink. What about a Coke?"

"Swell," I nodded.

"I've been putting away a lot of these," he said, getting two frosted bottles of Coca-Cola out of the icebox. "I'm trying to stay away from the hard stuff—at least when I'm at the studio."

"You tried to give up smoking last year," I reminded him, pointing to the pack of Chesterfields on the table.

"I've cut way down," he said defensively. "It isn't easy. Old habits die hard."

We sipped our Cokes and I looked him over. Dash was as

skinny as ever, a tall, lanky, elegant man with a shock of prematurely white hair that lent dignity to his angular face. His mustache, as always, was neatly trimmed, and he wore a freshly pressed white shirt with the sleeves rolled up. A pair of gray sharkskin slacks hugged his bony legs as he stretched out full length on the couch in his socks.

"I work better with my shoes off," he told me. "But that applies only to lousy scripts. Wiggling my toes helps when I'm working on a lousy script."

"I didn't expect to see you back here this soon," I said, taking a chair next to the couch. "What happened with Selznick?"

"What happened is, I quit," Dash said. "Selznick is nuts. Thinks he's Christ the Second. Worries about everything. Sends endless memos. Nothing anybody does satisfies him. Changes his mind ten times a day. Working for him on this desert disaster took years off my life."

I'd read about David O. Selznick's *Garden of Allah* in the Hollywood trade papers. Paramount had just finished *Trail of the Lonesome Pine*, which was the first outdoor picture to be shot in full Technicolor, so Selznick decided to use this expensive color process to enhance *his* film. The budget was enormous. He was paying Marlene Dietrich two hundred grand to play a mixed-up dame who goes to the Sahara in search of spiritual peace and ends up falling for a renegade Trappist monk played by Charles Boyer. Selznick sent his entire cast and crew to the Buttercup Valley in Arizona, sixty miles beyond Yuma, with the Mojave filling in for the Sahara. That's where Hammett had been for most of the last month.

"Were you hired to script the picture?" I asked him.

"No, no. They already had this god-awful screenplay when Selznick contacted me. He knew I'd worked with Dietrich on *Blonde Venus*. I was hired to supply her with on-set dialogue. Marlene likes to change her lines during production, and I was there to try and keep her happy. Kind of a literary whore."

"I hear she's a tough lady."

"Yeah. She can spit nails if you cross her."

"How'd the two of you get along?"

He grinned. "She's tough and I'm tough, so we got along fine."

He held up a printed sheet.

"What's that?"

"Some ad copy Selznick cooked up for this flyblown epic. Straight out of Horatio Alger." He began reading from the page. "Quote: 'The memory of barren, bitter years fell away. Nothing remained except the tropical stars, the silent desert night, and the tumultuous beat of their singing hearts.' Unquote."

"Wow. I see what you mean."

Hammett finished his Coke, setting the empty bottle on the floor next to the couch. He yawned, stretching both arms above his head. "Selznick sure put a lot of jack into this one. Even had a fake oasis built in the middle of the Mojave. With a giant pool, fancy tents, and imported palm trees. It actually looked great, except the whole shebang kept getting hit by desert storms. The pool would fill with sand, the trees would blow over, and all the tents would go sailing off in the wind like big kites. Each time, the production crew would put it all back together again. Meanwhile, Lady Marlene is prancing around in flowing silk gowns and high heels, with Boyer panting after her."

"Doesn't he wear a hairpiece?"

"When he can keep it on, he does—but the wind kept lifting it right off his scalp." Hammett chuckled. "He'd go chasing after his hair, wading through the dunes and cursing Selznick with every step. Generally, he was in a foul mood. But we all were. Sand in your coffee, sand in your ears, up your nose, in your mouth, down your shorts. You just couldn't get away from the stuff."

I had turned to face the window, listening to Hammett, when I saw a white limousine pull to a stop in front of Soundstage 6. A tall woman in a red dress, wearing a large picture hat, got out of the car, nodded to the driver, and began walking toward the stage entrance.

"It's *her!*" I exclaimed. "The weird character I saw at Julian's burial."

Hammett joined me at the window. "She's weird, all right. That's Carmilla Blastok. Claims she's a Hungarian countess."

"Is she?"

Hammett snorted. "Hell, no. Her real name's Letty Knibbs, and she's not from Hungary, she's from Newark. Her mother was a barmaid with three ex-husbands on the string and her daddy worked in a New Jersey meat-packing plant."

"How did she get tagged as a countess?"

"Don't you ever go to horror films?"

"Never," I said. "Cissy and I seldom go out to the pictures, and when we do, it certainly isn't to see horror."

"Well, kiddo, this dame has starred in a whole *slew* of 'em. She got going in the silent days with a series of Dragon Lady pics. When sound came in, she switched to playing vampires. Her first talkie was *The Blood Countess*, for Universal, which was a big hit. That's when she started telling everybody that she really *was* one, a genuine Hungarian countess—a kind of female Lugosi."

"Him I've heard of. Ole Dracula himself—Bela Lugosi."

"Right."

"And I saw Boris Karloff in *Frankenstein*." I shrugged. "But that's about the extent of my acquaintance with horror."

"Well, take my word, in fright-film circles Carmilla is the Vampire Queen. Or was. She retired from acting three years ago."

"How come?"

Hammett shrugged his thin shoulders. "She never said. Now

47

she just 'consults.' When a major bloodsucking epic is underway, the studio calls her in for 'occult expertise.' "

"Do you think she knew Julian?"

"Maybe. Easily could have."

"During the burial ceremony she was standing off to one side, playing it veiled and mysterious. When she saw me notice her, she hopped into her limo and was gone." I hesitated. "Do you know her personally?"

"*Know* her? Hell, Ray, I've been on this vampire thing for just two days and already she's driving me bats—to use an apt phrase. Global brought her in as consultant, and I have to listen to her spouting all this crazy stuff about 'the Undead.' The Countess is a royal pain in the ass."

"I need to talk to her," I told Hammett.

"Why?"

"To find out the reason she attended Julian's burial. She may know something about his death—something important. Will you introduce me?"

"Sure, no problem. Lemme put on my shoes and we can go over to Stage 6 right now, if you want to."

"I do," I said. "I most definitely do."

FIVE

On the way to the soundstage I asked Hammett: "How come she's here at the studio today?"

"They've built a full-sized family crypt, and the producer wants Carmilla to check it out for authenticity. You know, to see if it's dank and gloomy enough. That sort of crap."

When we were about to enter, the door burst open and a man in white swept out. He seemed electric with energy, moving with grace and purpose. He wore an all-white suit, topped by a white bow tie and a white, wide-brimmed panama hat. He was young, soft-faced but handsome, with a sensuous mouth (unusual on a man) and dark, arresting eyes that were fixed on Dash. Me, he ignored.

"Christ, you're *Hammett!*" he exclaimed in a bass rumble. His smile was bright as a beacon. "What extraordinary good fortune—to run into you here! I'm just in town for the day, on business—be producing my own pictures soon—but I never expected . . . Well, by *damn!*"

Hammett looked curiously at him, saying nothing.

The man thrust out a meaty hand. "I'm Welles. Orson Welles. Heard of me?"

"No," said Dash. "Should I have?"

"Perhaps not, as yet," said Welles, "but the New York papers are going wild over my *Macbeth*. I'm directing it for the W.P.A. at the Lafayette in Harlem. Staging it myself. Savage, primitive emotion. All-Negro Shakespeare. Never been done. Voodoo drummers. Dancing witch doctors. My star is a black Barrymore."

"What does all this have to do with me?" Hammett asked with an amused smile.

"I'm a rabid fan of yours," declared Welles. "Your novels explore the dark heart of America. You dig into the roots of societal corruption. I rate you with Dostoyevsky."

"That's nice to hear," said Hammett, "even if it's rather extreme. Is there a point to all this fulsome praise?"

"Indeed there is! To put it in simple terms, I want to stage your *Dain Curse* as a gothic musical."

"A gothic musical?" Hammett chuckled. "That's quite a switch."

"Exactly. I take pride in giving the public what they don't expect to get." He hesitated, frowning. "At the moment, in this Depression era of ours, I am rather short on personal funds, but this condition is only temporary I assure you. Unhappily, the fact is that as we speak I do not have the money at hand with which to option your book—but *Macbeth* is bound to launch me as a major force in theatrical circles. When this happens I'll be able to—"

"How old are you, Mr. Welles?"

"An odd question."

"I tend to ask odd questions."

"Well, I'm happy to answer you. I'll be twenty-one next month."

Hammett nodded. "Come back and see me when you're thirty."

Welles flushed beneath his white panama. "I'm no callow young fool. I know precisely what I'm doing. I daresay you are passing up a golden opportunity."

"I daresay I am," said Hammett, "but what I said stands."

Welles stiffened. "You severely underestimate me, Mr. Hammett. I made my stage debut as an actor at the age of three, with the Chicago Opera. At ten, I was adapting and directing. I wrote my first musical review at eleven. At fourteen, I was playing Marc Antony in *Julius Caesar*. I was doing Shaw at fifteen. At sixteen, I joined the Dublin Gate Theater Company in Ireland to pursue a host of starring roles. Two years ago I became involved with radio and I have now performed on a wide variety of top programs. I design costumes, produce, direct, play the piano, and paint my own stage sets. There is a greatness in me, Mr. Hammett, a greatness that you cannot comprehend."

"Along with a fair amount of bull."

This time he laughed, a deep drum rumble. "Insults mean nothing to me. I happen to possess an unwavering belief in myself, in my future potential. A small ego begets a small man. A giant ego begets a giant. When I'm thirty, I'll be world-famous and beyond your reach."

"Then that'll be my loss," said Hammett. "In the meantime, I wish you luck as a major force in theatrical circles."

"I make my own luck, sir, so I am not in need of yours." And he swept away, a white force of dynamic, kinetic energy.

Dash grinned at me, shrugged, and opened the stage door.

We went in.

There were three standing sets that had been built inside the cavernous soundstage. No filming was in progress, but a number of technicians were at work, dressing each set. The first was an exterior for a Global Western, consisting of some fake fir trees, a grouping of papier-mâché boulders, and a carefully spread dirt yard surrounding a false-front bunkhouse—all of it framed by a fifty-foot painted backdrop of purple mountains under a cloud-flecked blue sky.

Two stagehands were leading a swaybacked mustang past the set when the horse relieved itself.

"Dammit, Sid," growled the taller of the pair, "just remember, it's *your* turn to clean up the horseshit!"

"Can't have horseshit in a Global Western," Hammett said to me as we walked past.

The second set duplicated the interior of a flashy New York apartment, with chromium art deco furniture, mirrored walls, and a painted view of the Manhattan skyline. In the rafters above the set, two electricians were adjusting beam lights.

The third set was the vampire crypt, built at the edge of a fake cemetery with slanted wooden headstones and lots of weeds and dead grass. The crypt was open on one side, for camera access, and looked suitably dank, gloomy, and menacing to me, with its fake cobwebs, fat rubber spiders, and ersatz mold. The area swarmed with set workers busily painting, plastering, and hammering, supervised by a tall, laconic drink of water in faded orange coveralls who was, according to Hammett, the production manager. He nodded to us, shifting a wad of chewing tobacco from his right cheek to his left.

Inside the crypt, checking out the cobwebs, was the Countess herself. Spotting Hammett, she walked over to him, extending a gloved hand. The heavily rouged face beneath her picture hat had seen better days; she was gaunt, with sunken green eyes the color of stagnant seawater. Her mouth was thin-lipped and wrinkled under a long, patrician nose.

"Dashiell, how *nice* to see you!" The voice was high and fluttery.

Hammett took her hand in a mock bow. "Carmilla."

"What are you doing out of your ivory tower?" she asked him. "I thought you were deeply immersed in our script."

"My script," Hammett corrected her in a mild tone, edged with irritation. "You are the consultant, *I* am the writer."

"My, my, but aren't we touchy today. Have you been drinking, Dashiell?"

"Only Coca-Cola," he said. He turned to me. "This is my friend, Raymond Chandler. He insisted on meeting you."

"How nice!" She gave me the same gloved hand to shake. "And what is it you do, Mr. Chandler?"

"I write lurid detective stories for *Black Mask*."

"Wonderful!" she said. "I *adore* detective stories. I'm sure you're very good at it."

"I'm sure I am."

Hammett broke into our exchange. "Hedda's just come in. She wants to see me."

An agitated woman, wearing a huge beribboned hat with magenta feathers, was gesturing from the door of the soundstage.

"Who's Hedda?"

"The gossip columnist," said Hammett. "Hedda Hopper."

"Oh, yeah. I've seen her stuff in the papers," I said.

"She keeps saying neat things about me in her column. Gets me fatter contracts. I'd better go talk to her."

He headed for Miss Hopper.

"I never liked that woman," said the Countess, watching Hammett go. "She failed to appreciate the art I brought to my films. Louella Parsons was much kinder to me. Did you know that I was a featured guest on her radio show?"

"That's nice," I said.

There was a moment of awkward silence. Then the Countess asked: "Are you seeking my autograph?"

"Actually, what I'm seeking is information on Julian Pascal. He . . . died very recently. I saw you at his burial. Was Julian a friend of yours?"

"I knew Mr. Pascal only in a very casual way," she told me.

"He composed the music for three of my films. But we barely spoke. We were certainly never friends."

"Then why attend his burial?"

She seemed uncomfortable with my question. "It was simply an act of professional courtesy. I was there to pay my respects to a deceased colleague."

I smiled, trying to look pleasant. "You'll pardon me, but I suspect there must have been another reason."

She drew back, arching a plucked eyebrow at me. "Are you saying that I am *lying*, Mr. Chandler?"

"No, not at all. I just sense that you're unwilling to reveal the full truth about why you were there."

She studied me for a long moment, weighing me, her green eyes probing and intense.

"I'm sorry if I offended you," I said.

"You seem to be a very *intuitive* man, Mr. Chandler. I should like to pursue this matter at my home later this evening. Would you honor me with your presence?"

"I'd be pleased."

"Say, at eight then. For cocktails. The address is on my card." She removed one from an Italian ivory leather purse and handed it to me. "Will this be convenient for you?"

"Very convenient," I said, handing her one of my cards in return.

"Splendid! Then I shall expect you at eight."

She returned to her crypt as I walked over to join Hammett on the far side of the stage. He was engaged in spirited conversation with the big-hatted columnist, who wore a fashionable tea-rose pink afternoon suit and a lot of jewelry.

". . . and, of course, Dash, you've heard the latest about Gable and Loretta Young?"

"Nope," said Hammett. "Fill me in."

"Well, it's just *incredible*, but it's true! It happened when they were snowbound together at the Mount Baker Lodge in Washington. On location for Willie Wellman's *Call of the Wild*, you know. Well, a truly passionate love affair developed between them. Amour in the snow! Clark got Loretta *pregnant*, can you believe it? She's taken a leave of absence from filmmaking—the cover story is that she's ill—so she can bear their love child. Deliciously wicked, don't you agree?"

"I thought Loretta was an avid churchgoer," said Hammett.

"Oh, she is! Indeed she is," nodded Miss Hopper. "She's practically a walking saint." The columnist lowered her thick lashes. "But even saints get hot pants."

Hammett chuckled. "You're a real card, Hedda. Where do you get all this inside stuff?"

"I have my sources," she said.

"When I was a Pinkerton we called them stoolies."

"Every house has dirt under the rug. I just find out where all the rugs are."

"You're one of a kind," said Hammett. "Louella Parsons can't hold a candle to you."

"Louella is *such* a bitch," declared Miss Hopper. "She's always trying to scoop me."

"I'd say it's tit for tat," Hammett replied, with a smile.

"Well, I must fly," she said, checking her gold wristwatch. She swung suddenly toward me. "Are you anyone I should know?"

"Definitely not," I assured her.

"Then I'm off."

And she hustled grandly from the soundstage as a small magenta feather from her hat drifted languidly to the concrete floor at our feet.

Carmilla's card listed her home at 2300 Glendower Road, which is in the hills above Griffith Park. I had to consult a city map to pinpoint the exact address in a puzzling crisscross of streets angling up from the flats of Hollywood.

The Griffith Park beacon shot its long finger of light into the inked sky as I eased the big Duesenberg around a particularly tight curve. All of the streets at this height were narrow and winding, which made me glad I didn't live up here. Dimly lit by high yellow arcs, they seemed better designed for horse and wagon.

I knew there had to be a special reason behind this night's invitation. The Countess wanted something from me; she'd sized me up as a man she could use. For what? Julian's death was leading me into a new adventure, and I looked forward to my rendezvous with mounting curiosity and not a small degree of apprehension.

I cranked a hard right onto Glendower and suddenly, out of the cloaking darkness, the house loomed ahead of me. I didn't have to check the address to know it belonged to the Countess. It was huge—a sprawling mansion of spires, massive leaded windows, and castlelike towers dating back to the turn of the century.

The perfect abode for a vampire!

The gate was open. I swung my car left into a long bricked drive fronting the house and braked to a stop.

A light bloomed in a lower-story window as I stepped from the car. I walked up to the wide stone entryway, halting abruptly at a deep-throated growl. I could feel the hairs on my neck rise.

"Quiet, Bruno! *Easy,* boy!"

Carmilla stepped out of the shadowed entrance, wearing an embroidered black silk evening dress, with a string of pearls looped into her dark hair. She gripped the leash of a giant gray mastiff whose bared fangs and slavering jaw bespoke serious menace. The hideous growl had not entirely abated; it was muted now, but nevertheless blood-chilling. I felt like Sherlock

Holmes on Grimpen Moor facing the Hound of the Baskervilles.

"Now, don't be a naughty boy, Bruno," admonished the Countess, slapping him lightly on the rump. "This gentleman is our guest."

The dog glared at me, fur bristling, lips drawn back, straining against its leash.

"I don't think he likes me," I said, still not moving.

"Bruno dislikes *all* strangers. A burglar attempted to enter the house last year and he tore out the man's throat."

"Somehow, that's not reassuring," I declared, my eyes locked on the hellhound. "I can't say that I look forward to having my throat torn out."

The Countess smiled, patting the brute's head. "Oh, Bruno won't attack you with me around. Since I'm alone here so much of the time, he serves as my bodyguard. You'll find he's very sweet once you get to know him."

"I'll take your word on that."

She gestured toward the open door. "Please to enter, Mr. Chandler. You'll be quite safe."

I stepped gingerly into a marble-floored foyer as Carmilla followed, Bruno trotting at her heels. He gave me another low growl, as if to say, I'm watching you, Buster, so don't make any funny moves.

I didn't intend to.

SIX

Carmilla led me down a wide, mahogany-paneled hallway into a sitting room smaller than Yankee Stadium. Heavy drapes of purple brocade were swagged across the tall bay windows. The room had several sturdy-looking antique chairs and a long pale yellow silk sofa piled with pillows big enough to smother a horse.

Bruno padded over to a small, tufted oriental throw rug and bellied down there, rolling a wary eye in my direction.

Behind a screen of hinged brass, flames danced and crackled from a massive stone fireplace.

"It gets chilly up here at night," said the Countess. "I like to keep a fire going."

She took my coat, then beckoned me toward a deep purple velvet chair.

"I have some splendid Napoleon brandy. How does that sound?"

"Sounds fine," I said, settling myself into the chair.

Left-handed, she poured from a leaded-glass decanter that Queen Victoria would have been proud to own, brought a crystal snifter of brandy over to me, then poured another for herself. She sat down in a matching velvet chair, facing me.

"Are you familiar with my work, Mr. Chandler?"

"Unfortunately, no. I don't go to the pictures much."

"Let me sketch in my background for you, if I may."

"Please do."

The Napoleon was indeed splendid, its color a robust crimson as my glass picked up the reflected flames from the hearth. The oiled glow of the brandy soothed me; I was able to relax for the first time since entering this house.

"I was born Carmilla Blastok in the village of Lukos in what is now southern Hungary, less than fifty miles from the border of Transylvania. My father was of noble stock and my mother also came from a noble background. I was very young, still a school-girl, when a group of touring gypsies put on a play at our local theater. Watching them, I was transfixed and knew, at that mo-ment, that I, too, must act. At fifteen, I ran away from home to join a theatrical troupe in London. By twenty, I had shipped off to America where I—"

I raised a hand, stopping her in midsentence. "I'm afraid I can't let you go on."

She was plainly astonished. "But in heaven's name, why not?"

"Because what you're telling me is utter bunk. I happen to know that you're from Newark, New Jersey, and that your birth name is Letty Knibbs. Your father worked in a meat-packing plant. So you needn't try to impress me with all this flapdoodle about your royal Hungarian background."

"Who told you my real name?" She was angry, and plainly shocked.

"I got that from Hammett. Where he got it, God knows. Maybe from Hedda Hopper. Let's try being honest with each other. I don't give a damn where you were born, I only care about why you were at Julian Pascal's burial. Will you tell me that?"

"In due course," she said, a defeated tone in her voice. "I

thought I had erased my past, that no one knew about my real background."

"None of us can erase the past," I said. "We can only try to improve the future."

She put down her glass and walked to the hearth.

"You're very direct, aren't you, Mr. Chandler?" Her back was to me and the firelight haloed her hair.

"If that means I try to cut through lies to reach the truth, then you're right." I hesitated, watching her as she stared into the flames, unmoving. "Are you ready to say why you invited me here tonight? It wasn't just about Julian. You had another motive for the invitation."

"Direct . . . *and* intuitive," she murmured. Carmilla turned from the fire, having made a decision. "Please, follow me."

She nodded to the shaggy mastiff, who was watching us with a bright, alert stare. "Bruno, *stay!*"

We left the sitting room, walked silently down another hallway, which was hung with hunting tapestries, and paused before a heavy oak-paneled door. She opened it.

"My Room of Life," declared Carmilla.

I stepped inside to face an impressive display.

A series of gaudy film posters occupied the near wall. In front of them, a row of costumed female mannequins stood in frozen wooden postures, each in a costume worn by Carmilla for one of her various fright roles. Inscribed photos filled another wall, floor to ceiling: Karloff, Lugosi, Lon Chaney, Fredric March, Claude Rains . . . stars Carmilla had worked with in her various productions.

A tall, dark red cherrywood bookcase held awards and scrapbooks; on its top shelf were two dozen film scripts bound in tooled morocco. In the center of the room a film projector faced a grained white screen, with several large round metal film canisters stacked on the floor. A long beige davenport with fat leather cushions had been placed just in front of the projector.

"This is where I come to watch my life," said the Countess. "I refer, of course, to the films I made. They *were* my life, Mr. Chandler. Everything else has been cruel illusion." She gestured dramatically toward the wall of posters. "There!"

Each of them was emblazoned with the words:

STARRING THE

COUNTESS OF BLOOD

CARMILLA BLASTOK!

The painted images were ominous and gory, with the Countess hovering over her terrified victims, her green eyes alight with fire, daggered teeth revealed in a smile of triumphant evil. The titles were suitably grotesque: *Bride of the Devil Bat, Spawn of Dracula, Curse of the Vampire, Crypt of the Undead, . . .* and, of course, *The Blood Countess.*

Carmilla indicated a voluminous night-black bat cape displayed in a full-length glass case on the wall. "I first wore this in *The Blood Countess.* It was made for me by the costume department at Universal from my own design. I wore it in all my subsequent films."

"Impressive," I said.

She turned back to the posters. "In particular, I wish to call your attention to this one."

I drew in a breath. *The Dragon's Daughter*—the picture Cissy had called Julian's "Chinese experience."

I examined it. "But this isn't one of your films," I said, turning to her. "Why do you have this poster on the wall with the others?"

"When I began my career in the silents," she said, "I starred in a highly successful series of pictures in which I portrayed a character called 'The Dragon.' Absurd silent film melodramas . . .

61

ridiculous, really, but they paved the way for my later career. When sound pictures came in, the producer wanted me to continue with the series, but I refused."

"Why?"

"Because I was offered substantially more money to do *The Blood Countess*. It was my first vampire role—and after that, I played *only* vampires."

"Didn't you ever want to do something different . . . to extend your creative range as an actress?"

"Never. The Undead have always fascinated me. These prowling creatures of the night offer splendid dramatic possibilities. I have never regretted playing them. I am proud to say I was able to give them depth . . . dignity . . . humanity."

I looked at the poster of *The Dragon's Daughter* again, noting that the star was Elina Blastok. "Are you related to her?" I asked, pointing to the name.

"She's my younger sister. Actually, she's my only surviving relative. Everyone else has died." She smiled ruefully. "That's why I thought I could recreate my past, make it more . . . *dramatic*. Only Elina knew the truth."

She sighed, and then went on with her story: "As a child, my sister had a fairly successful career of her own in silents, as Elina Knibbs. But with the advent of sound, Elina needed to reestablish herself as an adult actress. The producer of my Dragon series got what he thought was a brilliant idea. He signed Elina in my place and had her change her last name to Blastok for audience identification. Thus, for publicity, *she* became 'The Dragon's Daughter.' "

"Was the picture a success?"

She laughed. "Oh, no! It was a box office disaster. A total failure. People were walking out in the middle, and the critics tore it apart. The producer blamed Elina and it ended her career. She never made another film."

"Are you aware that Julian Pascal wrote the music for *The Dragon's Daughter?*"

"Of course. That was the beginning of it."

"Of what?"

"Of Elina's relationship with Pascal," she stated. "They became dear friends. In fact, I suspect they became much *more* than friends."

"Are you saying they were lovers?"

"In my opinion, yes. But Elina would never admit such a thing to me. When I asked her, she denied it."

"What about *you* and Pascal?"

"I barely knew the man. He went on to do the music for *Spawn of Dracula* and two of my other films, but we were never more than working acquaintances. I'm sure he sensed my strong disapproval of his relationship with Elina."

"If you barely knew him, as you say, then I ask you again— why were you at Julian's burial?"

"I was hoping that Elina would be there . . ." The Countess hesitated, gathering her thoughts. "I've been searching for her without success."

"When did you see her last?"

Carmilla walked over to the big davenport and settled against one of the leather pillows, staring at her hands; the nails were long and vampire red. "It's been at least three years."

I sat down next to her. "Were the two of you close?"

"Very," she replied in a soft tone; her voice held sadness. "We were so much more than sisters. We were as one flesh, one soul. I have never been so emotionally involved with another human being."

"Did she live here with you?

Carmilla nodded. "I was making a lot of money from pictures. Elina was still very young when our parents died. I went to New Jersey to get her, brought her out here. She wanted to act, so I helped her get into the business. The camera loved her. She had a kind of sweet vulnerability that registered strongly on the screen. Elina became a child star almost overnight." The Countess paused, breathing deeply. "We had a very happy life together."

"What happened to separate the two of you?"

"When her acting career ended, my sister became extremely depressed. She hated living on my money, and three years ago last month, she left me for an utter scoundrel." Carmilla's eyes flashed. "I couldn't believe she was capable of such incredible misjudgment. We had a violent quarrel, each of us saying terrible things to the other. She left the house that same night, and although she called me once from a pay phone a month later, I haven't seen her since."

"I'm sorry it ended that way."

The Countess stared at me; I could feel the heat of those deep green eyes. "You sensed that I had a special motive for inviting you to come here, and you were quite correct. Mr. Chandler"— she put her hand on my arm—"I want you to find Elina."

"*Find* her! She's of age, isn't she?"

"Yes, Elina is twenty-two."

"Then she has free choice. If she wants to run off and live with some creep, it's really not your concern. You can't force her to see you."

"I don't intend to force her to do anything," Carmilla declared. "But I *must* know if she is alive. I need to know that she's safe."

"Why wouldn't she be?"

"The man she was involved with . . . he was very volatile. She admitted to me on the phone that he had beaten her. He's a monster, I assure you. I need to know that Elina is all right."

"Even if she *isn't*," I pointed out, "it's her life and *her* choice in men. Finding her won't change that."

"Of course, what you say is true," she said, a desperate note in her voice. "But I'm going crazy with worry! I will never have peace of mind until Elina is found. I won't bother her. I swear I won't. I just want to know she's all right."

"Check with the police. Maybe they can locate your sister."

"Elina has committed no crime. She's not a fugitive. I can't go to the police."

"Then hire a private detective. I'm a *writer*, remember?"

She spoke rapidly now, with firm conviction. "Private detectives can't be trusted. They're grubby little men who peep through keyholes and then, for all I know, sell the information to people like Hedda Hopper. I want *you* to find my sister, Mr. Chandler—and I'll make it worth your while. Find her, and I'll pay you a thousand dollars."

The sum rocked me; Cissy and I could certainly use the money. I hadn't been able to make a living wage from pulp writing, and our oil stock wouldn't last forever. But there was another strong reason to pursue Elina Knibbs. She might be able to shed light on Julian's death, having been as close to him as she once was. I needed to ask her some questions.

I told Carmilla I'd do it. "But let me get this straight. All you want me to do is find your sister and verify she's alive and well."

"Yes, that's all. I won't try to convince her to live here with me again. She can go on with her life, for good or bad."

She moved to her purse, extracted five crisp one-hundred-dollar bills, and handed them to me. "Take this now, Mr. Chandler. If you can't find Elina, it's yours to keep. Otherwise, I shall be happy to pay you the remainder of your fee when you have found my sister."

I thanked her, putting the bills away in my wallet. It seemed very strange. I'd written this scene several times—detective gets advance from eccentric to do job—and now it was actually happening to *me*. I felt very "fictional" at that moment.

"Have you had any contact with your sister in the past three years? Letters? Phone calls?"

"No, after that first call she never wrote or phoned again, and I had no way of knowing if she had remained in the Los Angeles area or, perhaps, had left the state. Then, about a month ago, I received a telephone call related to her."

"How do you mean, 'related'?"

"It was the man she'd run off with, Merv Enright. I recognized his voice immediately."

"What did he say?

"He said that Elina had asked him to get her jewelry back. When she went away with Enright, she'd left it here. Nothing spectacular; a few nice pieces—most of them from our family, passed down to her through inheritance. There was a pearl necklace—not very valuable, since the pearls were not of top quality—some rings, a bracelet, a broach. The best piece was an antique rose-gold watch. But even with the watch, I doubt that the lot would fetch more than a few hundred dollars."

"What was your reaction?"

"Of course I asked to speak to Elina, but he refused. He claimed she had nothing to say to me. That was painful to hear. I was on the verge of tears."

"What about the jewelry? Did you agree to send it?"

"Yes, I felt I had no choice. What if she were in trouble and needed the money? I know that Enright was in very poor financial shape when they ran off together. I couldn't refuse to help."

"She might have walked out on him long before. He could have been trying to con you out of her property."

"I knew that was possible, of course. The man is capable of anything—but I felt I had to take the chance that he was telling me the truth about Elina's wanting her jewelry back. After all, it *did* belong to her."

"So what happened?"

"He gave me an address and I mailed the jewelry according to his instructions. I went there, to the mailing address, thinking maybe I would find my sister."

"But you didn't find her."

"No. The address turned out to be nothing more than a mail drop. He'd already picked up the package by then and there was no way to trace him."

"Tell me everything you know about Enright."

She stood up, pacing uneasily as she talked, her eyes reflecting the hatred she had for the man who had "stolen" her sister. Naturally, she painted Merv Enright in very dark colors.

"Elina met him when she attended a local stage play. He had a small part in it. They went out to dinner together after the performance. He charmed her, telling her he was going to be a famous actor. And the silly goose *believed* him!"

"What was the name of the play and where was it staged?"

"It was by O'Neill—*Anna Christie*—put on at a small theater in Pasadena called Center Stage Left, by a group of amateurs who billed themselves as 'The Thespians.' Elina thought they were quite good."

"Did you go there and talk to any of them about Enright?"

"No. Elina told me he'd quit the stage, and so the idea never entered my mind."

"Did he tell your sister what he'd done before he got into acting?"

"He claimed to have been a real-estate agent in Colorado, but that's probably a fabrication. And he also said something about the war, that he'd served overseas in 1918."

"How old is he?"

"Midthirties, I'd guess. Possibly older."

"When did *you* meet him?"

"I met the man twice. Once when he came to the house to pick

67

up Elina—and again on the night she left. I took an instant dislike to him. He made no pretense of civility. He was rude and sullen. When I warned him, on that last night, not to abuse my sister, he just laughed at me, saying he'd take care of her *his* way. The man is a savage brute!" She abruptly turned toward me. "Oh, and I must tell you about his eyes."

"What about them?"

"They're shifty. Like the eyes of a fox. You can never trust anyone with eyes like his." She hesitated. "The eyes, as you well know, Mr. Chandler, are the windows of the soul."

"Do you have a photograph of him? And of Elina?"

"I have a shot of them both together. I believe it was taken by another actor. Wait a moment and I'll get it."

As she left the room I leafed through one of her fat scrapbooks. Full of clippings on her films: an interview from *Silver Screen* . . . publicity stills with her playing vampire for the camera . . . news items about premieres she'd attended . . .

Then she was back with the photograph. It was a shot of Elina and Merv standing arm in arm in front of the playhouse in Pasadena. He was small but thickset, with dark hair and a tight, mean-looking mouth. His face was narrow, and I could see what Carmilla meant by the shifty eyes. He *did* look something like a fox. Elina was quite striking, just this side of beautiful, with long blonde hair down to her shoulders and a pert, heart-shaped face. Her eyes were large and merry.

"May I keep this?"

She nodded. "Of course."

"What if she wants nothing to do with you? Can you accept that?"

"I'm sure Elina is still very angry at me for attempting to turn her against Enright, and I can indeed accept whatever outcome your search may provide."

"And you really think the two of them are still living together somewhere in the Southern California area?"

"Yes. I'm sure that when you find Enright, you'll find Elina."

"*If* I find him. I don't have much to go on."

"You'll succeed, I know you will," she told me. "I'm a shrewd judge of character, Mr. Chandler, and I rate you as a remarkable man. I have great faith in you."

"I'll try to justify it," I said. "But you've got to understand, the odds are—"

"*Damn* the odds!" she cut in, her diva's voice as sharp as a honed razor. "Just find Elina!"

I said good-bye to Bruno on my way out, but he continued to glare at me, showing his carnivore's teeth.

Obviously he was no judge of character.

SEVEN

Cissy was intrigued by my visit with Carmilla and was in full agreement with my decision to try to locate Elina. She was pleased with the unexpected money ("Maybe you should become a private detective, Raymio!"), but her primary concern was, of course, in clearing up the mystery surrounding Julian's death. Cissy still firmly believed it was murder. I was uncertain. Despite my strong feeling that Julian would never commit suicide, the facts seemed to indicate otherwise. But whether suicide or murder, Elina might provide a key to the mystery.

The next morning I met Hammett again in his bungalow at Global. He was curious about my evening with the Countess.

"I've never been invited over to her spook palace," he said. "You're lucky she didn't turn into a bloodsucking bat and go for your neck."

"She's not as eccentric as you might think," I told him.

"How about neurotic?" he asked. "You can't deny she's neurotic."

"All actresses are neurotic," I said. "Comes with the profession. They all crave public adulation. She's no worse than others I've met."

Hammett smiled. "Sounds as if you actually *like* the lady."

"I don't *dislike* her," I admitted. "Right now she's a lonely woman with a lot of pain in her life."

"Well, she's sure put a lot of pain into mine," Hammett declared.

He moved to the desk to pick up a stapled outline, waving the pages at me. "They want me to turn this into a shooting script," he said bitterly. "And guess what? The Countess, as official studio consultant, gave this piece of fly dung her personal okay."

Hammett sat down on the couch next to me, flipping through the mimeographed pages. Then he paused. "Care to hear some of these golden words?"

"Go ahead."

And he began reading:

> The terrified young virgin is running frantically through the dark woods, her dress ripped and torn, her eyes bulging in stark fear. She flings her body forward, driven by a sense of headlong panic. Now her foot catches on a root and she falls heavily to the leafy earth, striking her head sharply against a fallen tree trunk. She is stunned. Slowly regaining her senses, she looks up and screams! A dark figure is looming over her in the moonlit night. The figure is dressed in black with burning red eyes like a pair of hot coals in the darkness. He wears a long black cape and now spreads the cape over the trembling girl, enfolding her as in the grip of gigantic batwings.
>
> "What . . . what do you want with me?" the quivering young virgin asks. The figure emits a cackling laugh, lips drawn back from his sharp fangs. "I intend to drain the crimson fluid of life, the elixir of immortality, from your helpless body and make you as I

am—a creature of eternal darkness—a haunter of the night. You will awaken as a member of the Undead."
And, with fiendish delight, he plunges his sharp fangs into her tender young neck.

Hammett tossed the outline to the floor. He was scowling. "My God, Ray, it's the hoary old chase-through-the-woods scene that's about as fresh as ten-month-old hamburger. And the Countess thinks this is great stuff! When I told the producer I was throwing out the entire sequence and writing a new one without all the clichés, he said absolutely not—that Carmilla *loved* the scene and that it had to stay in the picture." Hammett groaned. *"This* is what she does to me!"

"Look, Dash," I said to him, "it was your choice to become a scriptwriter for Global. Nobody put a gun to your head. I say, just grit your teeth and *do* it. Quit fighting the front office and give them what they want. You're not doing *The Maltese Falcon* here. It's just a cheap vampire thriller. Why agonize over it?"

Hammett's face suddenly darkened and there was a stricken look in his eyes. "Maybe it's all I *can* agonize over," he said. His body seemed to lose substance, folding in on itself. "I've been trying like hell to get another book going. For three years I've been trying—but I can't seem to get the right words on paper. I tear up everything as soon as I've written it."

I didn't know what to say. The mood had turned oppressive; I'd tapped into an area I'd never meant to enter. I knew that Hammett had been having trouble getting a new novel under way, but I wasn't aware of the severe frustration he was suffering. To help cover the awkwardness, I launched into my account of what had happened the previous evening at Carmilla's house, ending with the assignment I'd taken at her request.

"And you figure that locating this Enright guy will lead you to Elina?"

"I hope so."

"Do you really expect to find him?"

"If he's still in Los Angeles," I said.

"And what if you do manage to track him down, but he's no longer with her. What then?"

"Then I'll try to find out when she left him and where she went."

Hammett sighed. "Sounds like a wild-goose chase to me," he said. "But if you want some help, I'm willing to give it."

"How can you help?"

"That acting group in Pasadena the Countess mentioned— The Thespians—where Enright met Carmilla's sister."

"What about them?"

"I know somebody who acted with the group. Roberta Haining. Bobbie. We went together for a while a year or so back. She has a wild sense of humor—and a very spiffy pair of gams. Bobbie might be able to give you a lead on Enright."

"You think she's still with the Pasadena group?"

He shrugged. "Last time I heard from her she was. We can drive over there and find out."

"When?"

"Why not now?" asked Hammett. "I've done enough agonizing for today. Buddy was going to pick me up here at the studio, but I'll tell him I'm going with you. Then, after we're through, you can drive me home. Okay?"

"Sure. Fine."

Hammett picked up the phone to make the call. "Buddy" was Hammett's nickname for his Haitian chauffeur. Dash considered his real name, Leonce Desvarieux, to be unpronounceable. Buddy was an obviously intelligent man who didn't usually say a lot, but once you got him talking, he had an inexhaustible supply of fascinating stories about his homeland . . . and its indigenous voodoo. It was something he didn't practice himself—in fact, he

73

disparaged those who did—but I suspected that, in truth, he believed in it more than he preferred to admit.

We were getting ready to leave when I felt an apology was in order. "About the script," I said. "I spoke out of turn. I have no business telling you what to write."

"Hey, don't worry about it, old sport. I'm the one with the problem."

"Old sport," I mused. "You've never called me that before."

Hammett chuckled. "Power of the printed word. I just finished rereading Scott's *Great Gatsby*. In the novel, Fitzgerald has Gatsby calling people 'old sport' this and 'old sport' that. Just stuck in my head."

"Didn't Paramount do a silent version of *Gatsby* in 1926?"

"Yeah," nodded Hammett. "Warner Baxter played him. It was lousy. Make a hell of a good talkie if they did it right. Now, that's a picture I *would* like to work on."

"Well, since we're going to Pasadena, I suggest we get cracking . . . old sport."

Hammett grinned at me, locked up the bungalow, and we headed for my parked Duesenberg.

We drove northeast out of Los Angeles toward the San Gabriel Mountains. It was a crisp clear day with plenty of sunshine from a cloudless azure sky that looked fresh-scrubbed. Southern California weather at its best. I wouldn't live anywhere else.

On the way, Hammett talked about his life in San Francisco during the early 1920s, and how he used to haunt the San Francisco Public Library, which was only a four-block walk from his apartment. It became his high school and college. I asked him what kind of books he read in those years.

"Everything," he told me. "All the usual classics by Melville and Dickens and Twain and Wells and Jack London. A lot of Henry James. And the Russians, of course: Dostoyevsky, Tolstoy, Chekhov. And, naturally, James Joyce. Plenty more."

"What about nonfiction?"

"Tons of it. I was particularly keen on medieval history and abstract mathematics. Baseball, too."

"And mysteries?"

He shook his head. "No mysteries. Not in the early Frisco years. I didn't want to be influenced by other crime writers. But after '27, when I was a professional book reviewer, I *did* read mysteries for *The Saturday Review,* and later, in New York, for *The Evening Post.* Most of them were stinkers, by people who didn't know what they were writing about. A lot of pretty sad stuff."

The playhouse in Pasadena, Center Stage Left, was on Colorado Boulevard, and I took San Marino Avenue over to Colorado. A large Spanish Mission–style stucco building with wood trim, it was set back from the street by a stand of heavy oaks. A tiled courtyard led to the entrance.

"They usually rehearse in the afternoons," Hammett told me. "At least they did when I knew Bobbie. The patio door should be open."

We walked under a blue-tiled Moorish arch, along a side passageway, to the patio door. Hammett was right; it was open.

Inside, we could hear voices declaiming Shakespeare. A wall placard announced:

OPENING SOON!
THE THESPIANS PRESENT:
A CENTER STAGE LEFT PRODUCTION OF
THE TRAGEDY OF
ROMEO AND JULIET

Quietly, we entered the theater's darkened interior. The stage was brightly lit and a costumed rehearsal was in progress. They were rehearsing the balcony scene. Juliet, a stunning petite blonde dressed in a long apple-green gown of the period, was leaning over the edge of a wooden castle wall, which had been painted to resemble stone. She gazed sadly down at Romeo, who was standing in a cardboard orchard.

In a voice breaking with emotion, she was pouring out her soul to him: "This bud of love, by summer's ripening breath, may prove a beauteous flower when next we meet. Good night, good night, as sweet repose and rest come to thy heart as that within my breast."

I whispered to Hammett: "That isn't Bobbie, by any chance?"

"Oh, no. Bobbie's a brunette, and she's a lot taller."

When the scene was finished, and the director called a break, we approached the assembled players on the stage and explained to them why we were here.

Bobbie Haining wasn't among the group. While Hammett went backstage to inquire about her, I asked the others if any of them had ever worked with Merv Enright. None of them had.

"There's a quick turnover here," the soft-faced young man who played Romeo told me. "You know, we're all amateurs, and nobody is getting paid, so if something better comes along, we take it."

"Bobbie Haining *was* acting here three years ago," said Juliet, "so she probably worked with Merv Enright. But she's not with us anymore. She left about eight months ago."

By now, Hammett was back. The director had told him the same thing: Bobbie Haining was no longer with the company.

"Where is she now?" I asked.

"In Rialto," said Juliet, adjusting her embroidered veil. "She's working in a bank there."

We thanked everybody and took off.

Rialto lies in the foothills, a good stretch beyond Pasadena in citrus grove country. For a while we saw nothing but oranges, grapefruits, and lemons; then the road twisted past a rail depot, a cannery, and various industrial buildings, with the green fruit groves eventually thinning away behind us.

We rolled on east, toward the shadowed foothills, climbing a fairly steep grade. As the road leveled at the top of the grade, an overhead sign formed an arch above a wide main street:

WELCOME TO RIALTO

A Little Town With Big Ideas!

It was typical of the smaller California communities nestled in this section of the state: quiet, tree-shaded, sparsely populated— with the usual cluster of grocery and clothing stores, a movie theater, a diner, two drugstores, and a big white wooden church at the end of the main thoroughfare.

There was only one bank in town: the Rialto Mercantile, in the center of the block next to a Woolworth's five-and-dime. It was late in the afternoon and the bank was closed.

"Now what?" I asked Hammett.

"The director at the playhouse gave me Bobbie's number," he said. "There's a phone in the diner. I'll call her from there."

She was home, agreed to see us, and told Hammett how to reach her place. I was relieved; it had been a long drive to Rialto.

"She sounds as sexy as ever," Hammett reported with a grin.

"Try keeping your libido in check," I told him. "We're going there for *information*, remember?"

"I'll be a good boy," Hammett promised.

Bobbie Haining's place was less than two miles east of town, where the road curved higher into the looming foothills. She lived in a modest frame house with an unkempt front yard given over to dandelions and crabgrass. Scrub oak dotted the hillside and the sharp scent of wild sage competed with the sweet smell of lilac in the clear air.

She was waiting for us by the open door, wearing a yellow shirt-blouse and black woolen slacks. Her thick brown hair was arranged in a French roll and her eyes were as blue as mountain lake water.

Hammett smiled. "Hi, darlin'," he said.

"My God, Dash," she said, "you're skinnier than ever! Don't you *eat?*"

"Constantly," he said. "It's just that food doesn't stick to my bones. I'm the original 'Thin Man.' "

He was about to give Bobbie a hug when a tall figure stepped out behind her. For a split second I thought it might be Enright, but the looks didn't match. This guy was football-big; even his face had ridged muscle along the cheekline, and his neck was thick as a tree trunk. Hammett was startled to see him.

"This is my husband, Don Fischer. We were married last month. I'm Mrs. Fischer now. Don, this is Dash Hammett, an old pal of mine, and you're . . ."

"Raymond Chandler," I said, taking her hand. Then I shook Fischer's beefy paw.

"Did Dash tell you why we're here?" I asked as Bobbie steered us into the house.

"Something about Merv Enright," she said.

"I'm trying to locate him. At the playhouse they said you might have acted with him . . . about three years back."

We sat down on some worn upholstered chairs in the living room. Don Fischer uncapped a cold bottle of beer, slouching in the kitchen doorway.

"Would you like some beer?" Bobbie asked. "Or I could fix coffee."

We said no thanks, we were fine. Then I asked her about Enright again.

"Yeah, I remember Merv. He came on hot and heavy to all the girls. Some of them liked it, but I didn't. I thought he was a

78

louse. And he couldn't act for sour beans. The directors kept giving him smaller and smaller roles, but he never got any better. Merv didn't even know how to walk across a stage."

"Would you know where he might be now?" I asked.

"Nope." She shook her head. "He finally got fed up and quit. Which was plenty okay by me." She frowned. "Like they say, good riddance to bad rubbish."

"What about the others in the group . . . the girls who knew him. Are you in touch with any of them?"

"Nope," she said again. "That part of my life is over. I had a lot of dopey dreams back then about how I was going to become a big movie star and all." She shook her head. "Dumb. Real dumb."

"Did Enright ever talk about his background—or his future plans?"

"Naw. Merv was real secretive. Didn't like people knowing anything about him. He never trusted anybody. Not anybody. He's probably left California by now."

"Why do you say that?"

"Because he never liked it here. Said it was full of phonies. Like that stage and film director, DuPlaine. They met at a dinner party once, and got into an argument about acting. Merv called him a phony. Hah! Pot calling the kettle black." She turned to Hammett. "How come you're so quiet, Dash?"

"Maybe that's because he don't cotton to me," drawled Don Fischer from the kitchen doorway. "Maybe he figured you'd just hop in the sack and spread your legs for him."

She whirled on Fischer. "You shut your dirty mouth! Dash and I had lovely times together."

"I'll *bet* you did," Don sneered, swigging the last of his beer. He tossed the empty bottle into the trash.

Hammett stood up, walked over to him, and then moved so fast I couldn't make out exactly what he did—except that

79

Fischer's left arm was suddenly twisted up behind him and he was groaning in pain.

"Lemme go!" he wailed. "You're breakin' the bone!"

Bobbie grabbed Hammett's sleeve. "Let him go, Dash. He didn't mean anything. Don just likes to wag his jaw."

Hammett released the big man, who stepped back, rubbing his arm. Dash said tightly: "When I was with the Pinkertons, I used to deal with assholes like you. Sometimes, I had to shoot off their kneecaps. That hurts a lot more." He hesitated. "Before she married you, Bobbie and I had a relationship which I happen to value. She's a good woman. She deserves respect, and I get very offended when I see someone who deserves respect not getting it."

"Okay, okay," whined Fischer. "I didn't mean nothin' by what I said."

Hammett walked over to Bobbie and kissed her on the cheek. "Bye, darlin'," he said, and left the house.

I thanked her for talking to me, nodded to Fischer, and followed Hammett outside.

The sun was westering. Our shadows were longer.

It was time to go home.

EIGHT

That night in bed I had a dream . . .

It was late afternoon in the dream. I was at home, working on a new crime novelette for Joe Shaw. About a showgirl whose life was in danger. She had become involved with the mob and had to be rubbed out because she knew too much. My detective shoots down a pair of hardcase professional gunmen, saving the girl's life. Lurid, fast-paced stuff. Shaw liked action, and I was giving him plenty. I even remember some of the overheated dream dialogue . . .

"You keep stepping on my toes, smart boy, and you'll end up in the drink wearing lead shoes and a concrete overcoat."

"You're a real kick in the pants. Now shed the heater and get your mitts up."

"Park it, sister."

"Take your paws off me, you big galoot!"

I remember all this because I wrote the words down in a notebook I keep next to the bed. Maybe I'll use some of it in future stories. Joe Shaw is a real sucker for tough lingo.

But, back to my dream . . .

As I was typing, hunched over the machine, really lost in the words, I realized that someone was seated in the big overstuffed armchair by the window—the one I do most of my reading in, usually with Taki snoozing on my lap.

I was turning slowly toward the chair, the way you do in dreams, when a familiar voice said: "Hello, Raymond."

It was Julian Pascal. Dressed the way he was the day we buried him. With the same bullet hole in his skull.

"You can't really be here, Julian," I said to him. "You're dead."

"I *know*. That's why I've come."

"What do you mean?"

"I wanted you to know that Cissy is right. I had no reason to kill myself. Life was good. I was composing some of my best music. I still had much to accomplish."

"You mean, you didn't—"

He leaned forward in the chair, his eyes narrowed. "It was set up to look like suicide. I'm a victim, Raymond. I was murdered."

I sat at my desk, dazed and not a little frightened. A part of me knew this was just a dream, but it seemed so *real*. I'd never talked to a ghost before.

"I finally bought the suicide," I told him. "Cissy didn't, but I finally did. To me, it read that way. And to the police, the same thing. Suicide."

He nodded. "That's what the killer wants everyone to believe. A lot of careful thought and planning went into it."

"Cissy never doubted that you'd been murdered," I said.

"God bless her!" declared Julian. "She's always been the great love of my life." He stood up. "Take care of her, Raymond. She's special. A treasure, that woman. One of the truly rare ones."

He was beginning to fade, becoming dim, the components of his body separating, misting apart.

I rushed toward him. "Julian! Wait! I have to know who killed you! Who *was* it? Who was your killer?"

"Take care of Cissy for me, Raymond. I've lost her forever now. God, how I'll miss her. My Cissy. Be good to her, Raymond. Love her . . . treasure her . . ."

And he was gone. Only a faint blue mist remained in the room. Then it, too, dissolved.

Which is when I woke up in bed, my silk pajama top soaked with sweat.

Cissy had also awakened. Her dark brown eyes were troubled. "What's wrong, Raymio? A bad dream?"

"No," I smiled. "A *good* dream. I believe you now—about how Julian died. He was here, Cissy. Here in this house, and he told me that you were right—that someone *did* kill him." I reached over, taking her in my arms, brushing her soft hair with my fingers. "And he told me how much he loves you."

Her eyes were brimming. "Oh, Raymio . . ."

I held her tightly, her head against my shoulder, and felt a wetness on my cheek. I tasted salt tears and realized they were my own. Cissy was so precious to me, so vital to my existence.

"Dear heart," I said softly, using our old term of affection. "My dear, dear heart . . ."

Cissy and I have never been much for neighbors. Not that we snub them, or that we're unfriendly; it's just that having moved so often, we make no attempt to establish personal relationships with whoever happens to be living next door to us. As very reclusive individuals, we have no desire to exchange empty neighborhood chitchat. Most of the time our privacy is respected, but on occasion a neighbor can be extremely annoying. Case in point: Mrs. Laverne Huttleman, who lives in the house to our east with Elwood, her blind parrot, and reads nothing but film star magazines.

A tall scarecrow of a woman, with narrow eyes, angular shoulders, a fleshy nose, and a widow's mouth as tight as a closed purse, Mrs. Huttleman gathers tidbits of neighborhood gossip the way a squirrel gathers nuts. We try to avoid talking to her whenever possible, but there are times when conversation is necessary. Such as the morning after my trip to Rialto when I had returned home from the local Market Basket. I'd just reached the porch with a sack of groceries and was fumbling for my key when Mrs. Huttleman leaned across the box hedge separating our yards and made a very odd remark.

Her voice, as always, was artificially cheerful: "I see you and the missus are coming up in the world."

I paused at the door, glancing in her direction. "Really? How so?"

"Well, I couldn't help but notice that you've hired a colored maid. She must be a great help around the house—what with your wife being so frail and all."

I stared at her, aghast. "Margaret Stetler is not our maid," I said, coldly spacing my words. "She is a remarkably talented concert pianist and a close family friend."

Mrs. Huttleman stiffened, drawing back; her face became flushed and her narrow eyes took on a hard, intolerant glare. She nodded curtly. "I see . . . Of course, it's none of my business, but—"

"You're right," I snapped. "Who we choose to have as a guest in our home *is* none of your business."

And I moved through the door, slamming it behind me.

Margaret was standing at the window. She turned as I came inside, smiling faintly. "I heard what the woman said."

"Never mind that old biddy," I told her as she followed me into the kitchen. I put the sack of groceries down next to the sink. "She's just a nasty-minded gossip."

"Uh-huh," nodded Margaret. "Well, she'll certainly have something to gossip about now."

I sighed, touching her arm. "I'm sorry."

"Don't be," she said. The morning light picked up the clean bronzed lines of her face. "It's no surprise. You know, when I was away on tour, performing for audiences who care about your talent, not the color of your skin, I had pride. I felt good about myself. I was a *human being*. But back here in the States . . ." She paused, drawing in a long breath. ". . . Back here, I'm just another Negro."

And there was nothing I could say to her in that ugly, painful moment of truth.

I phoned the Countess to report that I'd run up against a blank wall on the playhouse trip.

"You *do* intend to keep trying, don't you?" she asked me. "It's vital that you keep trying."

"I'm not giving up," I assured her, "but, as you know, I don't have any experience in running down missing sisters or scummy ex-actors. I'm sure I'll come up with something. I just need time."

She sounded relieved. "I still have supreme faith in you, Mr. Chandler. Please stay in close touch."

"I'll do that," I said, ending our talk.

It was her supreme faith that bothered me. I'd have preferred her to damn me for being incompetent; it would have eased the pressure. I didn't know if or when I'd ever find Merv Enright or Elina Knibbs, nor did I have any bright ideas on how to trace them. The situation was daunting.

Since my dream about Julian, I wanted to talk to Elina more than ever. If he *was* murdered, as I now believed, she might know something about it.

*　*　*

I drove over to seek counsel from Erle Gardner. The fact that Erle had been a practicing lawyer for many years gave me hope. Surely he could provide a tip or two on the art of locating missing persons.

When I got to the house, Gardner was just pulling out of the driveway in his camper. I left the Duesenberg and walked over to him.

We exchanged hellos, and he told me he'd been thinking a lot about Julian's death, wondering if I had picked up any more information about it.

"Not really," I said. "Right now I'm trying to locate a woman who might know something—which is the reason I came to you."

"Why me?"

"You were a lawyer. How do lawyers find people?"

"I used the cops. *They* find people."

"No good," I declared. "This isn't a case for the police."

Erle ran a slow hand over the steering wheel. "Well, look . . ." he said. "You caught me on the fly. I'm heading for the high desert in Antelope Valley. I plan to sit under a Joshua tree all by my lonesome and plot a Pete Wennick novelette for *Black Mask*. Then I have to outline my next Doug Selby novel, *The D.A. Calls It Murder*. Like the title?"

"Yeah," I said. "Sounds fine."

Gardner had so many characters going in his fiction that I couldn't keep track of them. I had no idea who Pete Wennick was, but Erle *had* told me about wanting to do some books about a small-town district attorney named Selby, so that name rang a bell.

"How long will you be gone?" I asked him.

"Two . . . three days at the outside. I just need a break. Those quacks over at Warner's have been driving me nuts with their phone calls. They want me to work on a Mason picture, and I keep telling them to get lost. Then I decided *I'd* be the one to get lost—that I'd just drive off into the Joshua trees where they don't have any damn telephones. So . . . like I said, you caught me on the fly." He hesitated, frowning. "I'd like to sit down with you and talk over your problem, but—"

"Hey, it's okay. I understand. Have a good trip, Erle."

He leaned from the window of his camper. "I don't know who you've talked to about this missing woman, but I can tell you that whenever I thought I was striking out with a witness, I'd go back over everything the person had said, looking for stray clues. You might try that."

"I'll keep it in mind," I nodded. "Happy plotting!"

"Thanks, pal."

He put the camper into gear and rolled out of the drive into the street. Just before he turned the corner at the end of the block, he waved.

I waved back.

A consultation with Hammett was in order, so I phoned him at the studio. He was finally cooking on his vampire script and seemed a little reluctant to leave it, even for a phone discussion. But I told him it was important.

"Dash, I need to put that detective mind of yours to work."

"*Ex*-detective." His tone was indulgent but frustrated. "How many times do I have to—"

"I know, I know. Just be quiet and listen to me."

"Yes, Mr. Chandler. Whatever you say, sir."

"And cut the horseplay. I'm serious."

"Aren't you always?"

"Are you saying I have no sense of humor?"

"God forbid. You're a regular laugh riot when you bust loose."

"This is getting us nowhere."

"You started it," said Hammett.

"I want you to help me remember something that Bobbie Haining may have said."

"Now that's a very ambiguous statement."

"I realize that she didn't appear to know anything of importance about Enright—but I seem to recall a reference to somebody named . . . De Penn."

"DuPlaine," supplied Hammett. "Bobbie said that Enright hated phonies like DuPlaine."

"Then you're familiar with the name?"

"Oh, sure," he said. "David DuPlaine. Bigtime director. Had a lot of silents to his credit before he got into sound. Also did quite a bit of stage directing—until he made it in films."

"I think I should talk to him."

"That'll be tough to pull off."

"Why?

"Because he died three years ago. Shot by a burglar who was robbing his house in Beverly Hills. I always thought there was something fishy about it."

"What do you mean?"

"Just a gut feeling that the story printed in the papers had more behind it."

"Based on what?"

"Based on nothing. Call it a hunch."

"Was DuPlaine married?"

"Not when he croaked, he wasn't. But he *was* involved with someone."

"How do you know?"

"Trade gossip. David was known for being a ladies' man. Tall, athletic, good-looking. Sharp dresser. Liked to spend money. Women fawned over him."

"Then you knew him?"

"No, not really. I saw him strutting his stuff at a couple of premieres and a party or two. But I was strictly an observer. Never talked to him personally."

"I'm going to look into this," I said. "Enright was involved with him in some way, and that's worth a follow-up."

"Fine," said Hammett. "Can I go back to my vampires now?"

I chuckled. "Thanks for the info, Dash."

"Any time," he said, hanging up.

Buddy appeared at our door about two hours later with an envelope for me. From Hammett. On the outside, he'd scrawled: "Thought you might want to see this."

It was a clipping from the *Times*—part of the regular front-page column by Irvin S. Cobb—and it concerned DuPlaine's death. Mr. Cobb speculated that "the burglar story" didn't ring true. But he didn't say why, and there wasn't much else to the column. At least it helped support Hammett's contention that something was amiss in the case.

Margaret, who'd been in the kitchen fixing a late lunch, had answered the door, and when I introduced her and Buddy I could sense an immediate chemistry between them. Her face changed almost instantly; grief and depression were replaced by a youthful joie de vivre that I hadn't seen since before Julian died. She was suddenly smiling like a schoolgirl, and Buddy was happily flustered. Usually, he was anything but animated, content to sit quietly behind the wheel of Hammett's limo and play the Good Chauffeur, but now he fairly *bloomed*.

"Buddy is not my real name," he told her in his soft French accent. "That's just what the Chief—Mr. Hammett—calls me."

"Tiens, comment vous appelez-vous?" Margaret asked with an insouciant smile.

I got the impression that Buddy had never before been so delighted to be asked his name. "Vous parlez français!" he exclaimed in delight.

"Certainement!" she said, her shoulders moving in an expressive Gallic shrug. "Et . . . comment vous appelez-vous?"

"Leonce Lebert Aurele Desvarieux, mademoiselle," he said with a bow. "D'Haiti."

"Margaret Stetler," she said in return, and to my amazement, she actually dipped her knee in a slight curtsy. "De Los Angeles."

"Je suis heureux de faire votre connaissance, mademoiselle," he said, acknowledging her introduction by extending his hand.

"Et moi, aussi," she replied, shaking it.

There was an awkward moment of silence. "Well, I guess I'd better be going," he finally said. "The Chief expects me back."

"It *has* been nice meeting you," she said, this time in English.

"Oui, mademoiselle," he said softly. He turned and left the house, closing the door behind him. Margaret, in a kind of happy daze, wandered back toward the kitchen.

Cissy had been watching the Buddy-Margaret exchange from the hallway. She joined me in the living room.

"Margaret was positively *glowing*," she said. "We have to do something about it."

"About what?"

"This is the first time I've seen Margaret smiling since she arrived. She needs cheering up," Cissy declared in that firm tone of voice that I knew so well. "We'll invite Buddy over for dinner. They'll have a chance to get to know each other." She looked at me intently. "Does Buddy have a girlfriend?"

"How would *I* know? I've never heard him mention one—but he's not much of a talker."

"He certainly talked to Margaret."

"Yeah, he did."

"All right, then, the sooner the better. What about tomorrow night? Let's see . . . I can cook sole *bonne femme* . . . a pineapple chutney—I hope they have pineapples in Haiti, I'm doing it for Buddy—chateau potatoes . . . a nice green salad with walnut oil and raspberry vinegar . . . and . . . what do you think about chocolate soufflé for dessert?"

"Sounds delicious."

"Good! Now, you're going to have to drive Margaret over to Van Rensselaer's; they'll have everything I need. I'll write a list—"

"Cissy! I've got work to do, and Van Rensselaer's is in Beverly Hills."

"Well, what exactly did you have planned for this afternoon?"

"I need to go downtown."

"That's perfect! Take Margaret along, and you can stop by Van Rensselaer's on the way. It'll do her a world of good to get out of the house for a while and I know she'll enjoy the drive."

"Buddy's day off isn't until next week."

"Dash won't mind. Just tell him we want to borrow his chauffeur for the evening."

"I think he'll go along with it."

"Of course he will. After you talk to Dash, tell Buddy we want him here for dinner tomorrow night at eight. Tell him we insist."

I grinned. "From the way he looked at Margaret, I'm sure that won't be necessary."

And Cissy grinned back at me.

I've written extensively about crooked cops, about police on the take, about the pervasive corruption extending from City Hall to the city streets. It's a nasty fact of life here in Los Angeles, and in many other cities, the sad result of the pernicious influence of money and power. But it's not the whole picture.

There are now, and have always been, certain cops who are

91

straight and honest, cops no one can bribe or buy off, cops you can respect, depend on, and admire.

Cops like Arthur Francis McQuillan.

I've known Art since the middle of 1933. I needed some pivotal background material for my first crime tale, "Blackmailers Don't Shoot," and a friend of mind told me to go see Captain McQuillan who worked out of downtown Central Homicide. Art and I hit it off right away. Not only did he supply the basic material I needed (which helped greatly in selling that first story to Joe Shaw), but he invited me to accompany him as an observer while he conducted homicide investigations for the city—a unique and welcome opportunity for a writer specializing in crime fiction. I saw Art in action on a number of occasions and can testify to his courage and personal integrity. He's tough, diligent, and resourceful, with a keen mind for detail.

Whenever I have one of my yarns printed in *Black Mask* I send him an inscribed copy of the issue. He tells me that he enjoys my stories, but that I go overboard on the melodrama. Too many blondes, too many guns going off, too much violence. Since Art has never been seduced by a wily blonde, been sapped with a blackjack, or needed to shoot a gun-waving psychotic, he thinks my stuff isn't all that realistic. Of course he's right, but total realism is not what Joe Shaw wants to buy. Seductive blondes, gun-happy punks, and private detectives with iron skulls are in demand. Melodrama sells. *Black Mask* is designed to entertain, and readers expect hard action. For me, it's a tightrope act between turning out the best fiction of which I am capable and meeting the demands of a commercial market.

We hadn't been in touch for a while when, with Margaret waiting downstairs in the Duesenberg, I showed up at McQuillan's Homicide Bureau office in City Hall on Spring Street to ask him about the DuPlaine case. I knew I'd get straight answers.

His office was in its usual condition: a mess. Case papers were stacked everywhere, on and under chairs, against the walls, and on top of a battered brown filing cabinet. I wondered if any of them ever made it inside the cabinet; maybe all the drawers were empty. I'd never looked.

Art's cluttered desk was a scarred oak relic with a clouded glass top. A cork-framed photo of his wife and three kids fought for space with piled folders, a plaster elephant he'd won at a carny shooting gallery, a fat dictionary I'd never seen him open, and a chipped wooden cigar box. He flipped back the lid and offered me a smoke. I declined.

Art always offers me cigars even though he knows full well that when I smoke, it's always a pipe.

He lit a dappled stogie, inhaled slowly, then expelled three perfect smoke rings. I watched them drift toward the ceiling. "So how's the writing game coming along these days?"

"Swell," I said. "I've been giving Hemingway fits. Got him real worried about me, poor guy. Guess he can't stand the competition."

The captain grinned, chewing on his cigar. "With your sense of humor," he told me, "you oughta write for Jack Benny."

I nodded toward the photo on his desk. "How's your family?"

"They're all okay—except that Clara's been ragging me to retire and I keep promising her I will. But the truth is, I'm finally getting the hang of this business. I'm actually beginning to know my ass from my elbow."

McQuillan was square and chunky in a shiny blue serge suit, with a pleasant, lived-in face and too much sand gray hair that kept falling across his eyes. He hated wearing glasses, but needed them to read.

He nodded toward the cracked leather chair facing his desk. I took it.

"Want me to guess why you're here?"

"Sure," I said. "Guess."

"You're in trouble with one of your bang-bang private eye epics and you need my professional expertise to bail you out."

"Wrong. I'm here about a shooting that happened three years ago. Film director David DuPlaine."

"Yeah, I remember the case," Art declared. "Going to use it for a story?"

"Could be," I said, "but I'm actually here to check out the guy. I'd like to see what's in the file."

"Sit tight and I'll go fetch it," McQuillan said. He paused at the door to fire another grin at me. "I figure all this is gonna end up in one of your stories and I should rate some credit." He spread his thick-fingered hands in the air. "Featured in *Black Mask* this month, 'The Director Bites a Bullet,' a new crime shocker by Arthur McQuillan and Raymond Chandler."

"Nice title," I said, "but the byline stinks."

Still grinning, he left for the department's file room. I sat tight until Art returned with a paper-clipped folder, tossing it into my lap. A tab along the top carried the case number and the name, DUPLAINE, DAVID B.

I opened the folder, studied the unsettling autopsy photos, and began reading the typed pages as Art lounged back in his wooden desk chair, puffing on his cigar, creating a line of perfect blue-white smoke rings in the air.

I was looking for a connection between DuPlaine and Merv Enright. I didn't find it. But I *did* find some information that startled me.

I looked up at McQuillan. "It says here that DuPlaine directed *The Blood Countess*."

"Then he must have," declared McQuillan. "I never saw any of his pictures. All that crazy spook stuff about blood sucking, people turning into bats, coffins, and stakes through the heart. My God, what crap! Give me a good upbeat musical like *Top*

Hat. You walk out of seeing a picture like that feeling great."

I scanned the remainder of DuPlaine's credits: *Bride of the Devil Bat, Spawn of Dracula, Curse of the Vampire,* and *Crypt of the Undead.* All starring Carmilla Blastok. In fact, every picture he had directed after *The Blood Countess* had starred Carmilla. Obviously, his name has escaped me on the posters I'd seen in her home. So I had a tie-in, all right, but not the one I had expected to find.

I glanced up at Art again. "According to this file, they never found the killer."

"That's right," he nodded. "Some two-bit house thief with a gun he never intended to use."

"How can you say that?"

"Stay in this game long enough and you get so you can read patterns. Burglars follow a pattern. They don't plan on shooting people. Lot of 'em don't even carry a gun. They look to get in, grab some loot, and skedaddle. When they pick a house to break into, they always make sure nobody's home. But DuPlaine suddenly turned up—an example of being in the wrong place at the wrong time—and walked right into the middle of the robbery. In panic, the guy shoots him dead, grabs the silver he'd been collecting, and takes off like a scalded skunk. We have no idea who the guy is or where he went."

"And that doesn't bother you?"

"Sure it bothers me, but there's nothing to be done about it. In cases like this, the killer almost always gets away. If DuPlaine had come home a half hour later, he'd likely still be alive. He should have gone to the premiere."

"What premiere?"

"They found a ticket in his coat pocket—for a Gary Cooper film premiere that night. But he never went."

"Why not?"

Art shurgged. "Who knows? It didn't seem important. The point is, our unlucky friend walked into a bullet, pure and simple."

"Pure and simple, huh?" I closed the folder, placing it on his desk. "Maybe *too* pure and *too* simple."

"Well, you can add some juice to it for your story."

"Yeah," I said, standing up. I told him I was grateful for his help.

"Don't forget to send me a copy when this one comes out."

"You bet," I said.

As I left, Art McQuillan blew a fresh, perfectly round smoke ring at the ceiling.

NINE

It was time to have another talk with the Countess. When I phoned, telling her that I had not yet been able to trace Merv Enright or Elina but that I needed to see her, she suggested we meet at a new restaurant she favored, the Blue Dove.

"It's between the Garden and Ciro's on the Strip," she told me. "I'll be in the bar."

I drove through Hollywood to the Sunset Strip, slowing as I passed the Garden of Allah Hotel. And there it was, on Sunset just short of Ciro's, marked by a high-flying dove in blue neon. I parked in a lot behind the building and walked through a heavy brass-bound door into the bar.

The area was dimly lit, but I spotted the Countess sitting with a man in a corner booth. Carmilla waved me over and I was introduced to her table companion, millionaire actor Charles Chaplin. As I shook his hand I was surprised to find that he was smaller than I'd expected, a solemn-faced little man with silver hair and sad eyes in a gray suit of English twill.

"We're having an excellent French Chablis," Carmilla told me, nodding toward her wine glass. "I recommend it."

"Fine," I said, and the waiter took my order.

Without his legendary bowler, black mustache, cane, and baggy pants, I barely recognized Chaplin. Of course, I knew a lot about him. For one thing, we shared a British boyhood. His early years in England, however, were far different from mine. Chaplin's mother was a music hall singer and his father was in vaudeville, so dramatic talent ran in the family. But before finding his place on stage and screen, Chaplin had endured a miserable, Dickenslike childhood, being shuffled in and out of workhouses, suffering from extreme poverty, seemingly destined for a life of hopeless obscurity.

At twenty-one he came to America and was seen on the New York stage by Mack Sennett, who brought him to California to begin his unique career in comedy at the Sennett Studios in 1913. By 1917 Chaplin was earning more than a million dollars a year with First National. In 1919 he helped form United Artists; he was soon operating his own Tudor-designed studio at Sunset and La Brea, smack in the middle of a lemon grove. He'd made *The Gold Rush* and *City Lights* there and was now one of the most powerful talents in Hollywood. I'd heard great things about his newest comedy, *Modern Times.* Sipping my dry white burgundy (Carmilla had been right; it was a superb wine), I told him how much I admired his talent, citing him as a comic genius.

"Comic genius, am I? That's what a lot of people have called me, but it's all timing and hard work. That's the secret."

It was somehow surprising to hear his voice since he had never uttered a word on screen. Chaplin disliked the "talkies" and in this era of sound refused to allow his film characters to speak. His voice was high and carried a slight British accent which was unmarked by any evidence of his humble origins. Indeed, I reflected, he would have fitted in splendidly with my old school chums from Dulwich.

"I'm pleased to say that Charles admires my films," declared the Countess.

"That I do," agreed Chaplin. "I am utterly fascinated by their impressionistic grotesquerie. They delve into the deepest recesses of the blighted soul."

"Mr. Chandler is a crime-fiction writer," Carmilla told the comedian. "Right now, as a special favor, he's attempting to help me locate my sister."

Chaplin was not interested in switching subjects; he ignored her words, keeping his intense gaze fixed on me. "Do you know anything about vampires?" he asked.

"Very little," I admitted.

"I am convinced that they exist today, in our modern world," nodded Chaplin. "Individuals who have the urge to drink human blood. More than an urge, a *compulsion*."

"Charles is correct," put in Carmilla. "The vampire is not merely a concept of the imagination."

"I find it difficult to believe that there are people who transform themselves into bats and sleep in coffins all day," I said.

"Ah, but you refer to the popular conception of such individuals," said Carmilla. "You judge strictly on the basis of what has been imagined in a *mythic* sense and not on the concrete reality *behind* those myths."

"The remarkable aspect of Carmilla's work in films," added Chaplin, "was her ability to transcend the vulgar common conception of the vampire and present such creatures within a painfully realistic *human* framework."

"I don't mean to be disrespectful," I said, "but this kind of talk strikes me as being a little nutty. I categorize vampires with Santa Claus and the Easter Bunny."

Chaplin stood up abruptly from the booth, tight-faced. He was glaring at me. "You are a fool, sir," he said, "and I do not enjoy the company of fools."

He bowed to the Countess, kissed her hand in courtly fashion, and walked out of the restaurant.

I shrugged. "Somehow, I don't think I charmed him."

Carmilla was not amused. "It's nothing to make light of," she said tartly. "Charles is a man of delicate temperament, and your words upset him."

"I was simply expressing my opinion."

"Well," she nodded, "be that as it may. Let us address the point of this meeting. On the telephone you said you needed to see me. Why?"

"I want to ask you about the man who directed your vampire films, David DuPlaine."

The muscles along her jawline tightened and she drew in a slow breath. "What is it that you wish to know about him?"

"Anything you can tell me," I said.

"You must have a reason for this. I'd like to know what it is."

"I think that DuPlaine's death may have something to do with Merv Enright," I told her.

"In what way?"

"I don't know yet. I need more information. Are you willing to talk about DuPlaine?"

"Why not? You'll find out about our relationship eventually."

"Relationship?"

"I speak in a professional sense, of course. David and I were very close. He was my artistic mentor, the center of my creative universe. He understood me as no one else ever has."

She removed an exquisite Indian-carved ivory holder from her purse, inserted a Gauloise, lit it with a jadeite-chased gold Tiffany lighter, and began puffing away nervously. It was clear that she did not enjoy discussing DuPlaine.

"He died three years ago. You retired from films three years ago. Is there a connection?"

"I found it impossible to continue acting after David's death," she said. "He brought an understanding and a sensitivity to my career that could be neither duplicated nor replaced. He shaped and guided me as a creative performer. It was simply impossible to go on without him."

"And what do you feel about the way he died?"

She tapped ashes from her cigarette into a crystal tray. "I don't know what you mean."

"The police think that a house burglar shot him. Do you agree with that?"

"It was obvious. David returned home earlier than expected and caught a thief in the act of robbing his home. He was killed by the man, who then escaped." She lowered her eyes. "It was a tragedy . . . a terrible thing. It devastated my life. But there's no question of how it happened."

"I think there may be," I said. "Around the same time DuPlaine was shot, Merv Enright left the theatre group in Pasadena to run off with your sister. And I know he didn't like Du-Plaine."

She was staring at me. "Are you suggesting—"

"What if Merv Enright was the one who shot him?"

"Why on earth would he do such a thing?"

"To get back at a man he envied. To hurt you."

She smiled thinly. "That sounds like a very far-fetched theory, Mr. Chandler. Do you have any proof?"

"Not a shred," I admitted. "Just a strong suspicion in my mind that Enright may be the killer."

"And how does all this help you find him?"

"It doesn't. What it *does* do is give me an unsettling feeling that your sister may be living with a murderer."

She leaned forward to stub out her cigarette in the ashtray. "What you're telling me is nothing more than wild supposition. It's that lurid crime-fiction writer's imagination of yours running amok. The thing you must do is locate this man, not make up fantastic stories about him. Find Merv Enright and you'll find

101

my sister. That's the job you accepted. Forget all this talk of murder. It makes no sense."

"All right," I said. "I'll put my theory on the back burner. But don't expect me to forget it. I'll find Enright—but I may be running down a very dangerous man."

Buddy was delighted to accept our dinner invitation, and since Dash was entertaining one of his lady friends at home that Friday night, he was just as delighted to have Buddy out of the Palisades house. The idea was to bring Buddy and Margaret together, but there was also a personal bonus in it for me: I would finally be allowed to see the "real" Buddy, the man behind the chauffeur's uniform whom I'd never had the chance to know. It was a rare opportunity and, truthfully, I had no idea what to expect.

No idea at all.

He showed up at our front door wearing a perfectly tailored charcoal wool suit whose workmanship I instantly recognized: Savile Row. His highly polished black leather shoes were obviously from some Italian atelier, and the watch on his wrist was a Patek Philippe. I made a quick mental calculation in dollars of the probable pounds sterling, lire, and Swiss francs he had paid for the outfit and shook my head in stunned disbelief. Either Buddy had a part-time job robbing banks or there was a hell of a lot about him that I had never suspected.

Margaret met him at the door in one of her classically designed concert dresses, emerald green velvet with a simple scoop neck. She wore a single rope of Cissy's pearls around her regal throat and she looked absolutely stunning. They made a very handsome couple.

We sat in the living room, drinking cocktails and eating hors d'oeuvres, and though Cissy and I actually contributed very little, the conversation sparkled. Hammett's Nick and Nora paled beside Buddy and Margaret, who seemed to want to know everything about each other.

"In what part of Haiti were you born?" she asked him.

"In the capital. Port-au-Prince."

"One of the things that I find most interesting," she said, "is that in 1804, after the slave rebellion, Haiti proclaimed its independence as the world's first free black republic. What a wonderful accomplishment!"

Buddy smiled. "I think you've been doing some research."

Margaret blushed. "Well, a little. I just *happened* to be passing by the library today, and I decided to look up Haiti in some reference books. I've never before met anyone from your country. Everything I read makes it all sound so . . . so *different*."

"*That* my Haiti most certainly is," he agreed.

"When the American occupation began in 1915, and the sailors and marines landed in Port-au-Prince, were you there then?"

"Oh, yes. Absolutely. I was seven years old. It was an amazing experience. At first, I was afraid of the Americans, but as I got to know some of them, I learned to admire them. To me, *they* were the ones who were different, from another world. They told me so many magical stories about this country." He paused, smiling to himself in remembrance. "By the time I was nine I had made a very big decision: Someday I would come to this country to live. A mighty ambition for a little Haitian boy, and it took many years before I could carry it out."

"What about your family? What did they say when you announced that you wanted to live in America someday?"

"They laughed; a silly child's fantasy. Our family has French roots, and they wouldn't have thought it at all odd had I said that I wanted to be a Frenchman someday. In fact, they would have been very proud. But an *americain? Très bizarre*, as my maman said. None of my relatives ever believed that I would actually do it."

"How did you finally come here?"

"By a very long route. After I completed secondary school in Haiti, it was necessary for me to go to France for university. That was as expected in my social class. I went to Paris, studied philosophy and French literature at the Sorbonne, and then returned to Haiti."

"Your family must be quite wealthy."

"Yes," he said simply. "We are *ancien libres*; in English you would say 'the old free.' We were Haitian mulattos, descended from unions between the original white French landowners and slave women. Because of their white ancestry, some of the mulattos received their freedom before independence in 1804.

"In the case of my own family, we are among the oldest *ancien libres*; by the time Haiti proclaimed her independence, *we* had already been free for well over a century, and my family already owned a great deal of land. We had legal freedom, and there was considerable wealth, but we were socially inferior to *les grandes blancs*, the white elite. *That* didn't change until after independence."

"How did you finally get to the United States?" Margaret asked.

"Four years ago, in 1932, I asked some American friends to help me obtain legal entry," he said. "They were happy to help, and I soon had my papers. At last I had realized my childhood dream: I was going to live in America."

He sighed. "It didn't take long for me to discover that my dream had been unreal. In Haiti, my family remains an important part of the aristocracy, one of the oldest, most influential families on the island. When I attended the university in France, there was no color bar, and I was treated by the French as any other educated man whose roots extended back to the French nobility of the Middle Ages. I had enjoyed a privileged position in Haiti, and I had been similarly privileged in France. But here in America all those things—family history, education, wealth, and position—they all meant nothing." He shook his head sadly. "I found out very quickly that here I was just another Negro."

Margaret visibly flinched as her earlier words to me echoed through Buddy. Her attentive smile vanished and the light faded from her eyes. His plight was painfully familiar to her.

There was a moment of silence as we all contemplated the heavy import of his words. Margaret finally seized the initiative: "So what did you do?"

"Well, because I had come here to the United States, I had yet another problem. My parents were not happy with my decision to be an American. They wanted me to change my mind—to live either in Haiti or in France—and so, toward this end, they decided that I would no longer have access to family money." He smiled. "For the first time in my life, I had no financial resources.

"I wanted to stay here, so I took any job I could find: I was a short-order cook, a handyman, a janitor . . . all very depressing. I even picked cotton for a while in Mississippi—and I don't *ever* want to do that again." He held out his hands. "Look . . . I still have scars on my fingers from the awful thorns on those cotton bolls." We all saw the tiny white puncture marks.

"Well, I finally asked for help. I phoned an American here in Los Angeles, a retired general who had served in Haiti during the occupation. He'd been close to my family since 1915. He knew the Chief—Mr. Hammett—and he knew Mr. Hammett was looking for a chauffeur. I took the train out here, met the Chief, and got the job."

Buddy took a deep breath. "Mr. Hammett has been very good

105

to me. I'm grateful; I know that I'm lucky to be working during the Depression. I know that I have a very good job," he looked at us for a long moment, "for a Negro."

We sat there in silence, deeply immersed in our own thoughts. Finally, Buddy looked at Margaret. "I'd like to hear about your life. Where did *you* grow up?"

"Right here in Los Angeles," she said. "I'm the result of a lot of history . . . a lot of family wanderings. It's actually sort of amazing how I ever got here.

"My father's family came from Texas, and before that they were house slaves on a big plantation in Alabama. The slave-holder's son decided to seek his fortune in Texas—when it was still Mexican territory—and he took my father's family with him as servants.

"My mother's family came from North Carolina. They were originally slaves too, of course, but along the way they managed to pick up a considerable amount of American Indian blood, and a fair amount of white blood as well.

"After the Civil War, when the slaves were set free, my grand-pappy served as a 'Buffalo Soldier,' a Negro soldier who was posted in the West. He met my grandma in Santa Fe. She was from a proud old conquistador family that traced its history back to Spain, and did *that* relationship ever cause a scandal! Well, the only way to deal with the heap o' trouble their marriage caused was to move a long distance away, so he and Grandma eventually headed for Southern California.

"It took them a few years to get here. My mother was actually born in Arizona, during the time when my grandpappy was working in the copper mines over there. When she was two years old they all finally moved to California."

She paused, thinking. "You know, I'm glad I'm a native-born Angeleno; I can't imagine being anything else. Despite everything, I love this city. There's a greatness here, you can *feel* it. All

106

these different people coming to Los Angeles from all over the earth, working toward a better future for everyone. Someday this is going to be one of the most important cities in the world, you just wait and see if I'm not right." She paused. "Maybe Los Angeles will someday even lead the way in race relations. Wouldn't that be a wonderful thing?"

Cissy passed the tray of hors d'oeuvres around and we helped ourselves to the miniature English savories that I like so much.

"Mr. Hammett says that you are a concert pianist," Buddy said.

"I see I'm not the only one who's done research," Margaret teased, and I could actually see a blush form on Buddy's café au lait–colored skin.

"Well, I just asked a *couple* of questions," he protested.

"That's because Mr. Hammett doesn't *know* anything else . . . am I right?"

Buddy looked at me. "Don't you have an amendment to your Constitution that says, 'I decline to answer on the grounds that it might tend to incriminate me'?"

We all laughed; it was wonderful to share a moment of lightness again.

"Yes, I'm a concert pianist," Margaret said, "although someone . . . dear to me just died, and with his death, my career may have ended as well." Margaret looked meaningfully at Cissy.

"When I was in grammar school," Margaret continued, "there was a white teacher there—Mrs. Hunt—who took an interest in me. She said I was very talented and decided to help me. She made certain that I had music lessons several times a week— as well as a piano to practice on. It was an old instrument that one of her friends no longer had any use for, but to me it was the most beautiful piano in the world.

"Mrs. Hunt made it possible for me to enter several competitions and appear at a number of public recitals. It was difficult.

107

Sometimes she would arrange an appearance, but when we arrived in person for the first time, the 'invitation' would suddenly disappear and I'd have to go home without performing. I tried hard to get used to the rejection but I really never did. It *always* hurt.

"When I was in high school Mrs. Hunt introduced me to Julian Pascal, the man who . . . just died. Well, at first he was simply another white man to me, and I didn't pay him much attention. I had *plans*, and they began with Juilliard in New York. It's by far the best music school in the United States, and I *knew* it was where I was meant to go.

"Well . . . somehow it never happened. Nothing specific I could ever put my finger on; it just didn't happen. And finally I realized that it was never *going* to happen; not in this lifetime, it wasn't.

"That's when Julian came back into my life. I'm sure Mrs. Hunt must have told him about Juilliard. In any case, he said that I was, in his opinion, tremendously talented, and that I didn't have to go to Juilliard. He arranged for me to take lessons from a master teacher, Alessandro Camiletti, a world-famous pianist in his day who had come here from Milan.

"Julian worked harder than anyone will ever know trying to help me. He was *determined* that someday I would have a full adult career.

"It was Julian's idea for me to go out of the country—to build an international reputation which he hoped would eventually help me here. So I made a personal appearance tour across Europe, and after that a similar tour across Canada, and I was *doing* it—I really was! And then . . . he died."

She looked up, biting her lips. "I don't know what I'm going to do now. Without Julian, I just don't know what I'm going to do." She started crying. Buddy put his arm around her shoulders and pulled her close, letting her cry it out. Cissy and I sat quietly, unmoving; we were outsiders, observers—witnesses to a special pain that our skin color allowed us to escape.

Eventually Buddy politely suggested that it might be time to eat dinner. The mood lightened considerably as Cissy's beautifully prepared meal appeared on the table. She had outdone herself and I was very proud of her. As we worked our way though the courses (with the salad following the main course in the French manner), the conversation turned from the personal to the philosophically abstract.

It began with a casual statement from Buddy. "I find it interesting being a black person in this society."

"Interesting!" Margaret frowned. "That's far too kind a word. Maddening is more like it. Or depressing. Or frightening. Any of these fit."

"I'm not attempting to downplay the problem of skin color in this country," said Buddy. "It's just that as an outsider, I am in a position to take a more objective view."

"Like Proust, you mean?"

Buddy looked startled. "How do *you* know about Proust?"

"When I was in Paris the people I was staying with talked a lot about him. So I bought a set of his books in English translation."

"Then you know that Proust was never truly objective," Buddy declared. "His work contained only the *illusion* of objectivity."

"But he recaptured precise psychological and sensory detail in recreating the French society he knew," argued Margaret. "He obviously possessed total recall."

"Yet he was, after all, a novelist," Buddy countered. "*Remembrance of Things Past*, however autobiographically precise, is still fiction. I'm speaking factually."

"What's fact for you may be fiction for me" said Margaret.

I didn't quite follow that, but she plunged on.

"Novelists often reveal deeper truths *through* their fiction.

Take William Faulkner. His portrait of race relations in the South, particularly in his native Mississippi, is absolutely accurate. You ought to know that, you picked cotton there!"

Buddy came right back at her: "But Faulkner's looking at it from a white perspective. He's bound to present a distorted view no matter how accurate he attempts to be."

"Are you saying that no white person can understand or speak for a colored person without distortion? That's ridiculous!"

Cissy and I exchanged amused glances, content to sit back and allow them to dominate the conversation, enjoying their spirited give-and-take.

By common consent, dinner lasted a long time. When it was over, Buddy graciously thanked Cissy for a "meal so exquisite it should be listed by the *Guide Michelin*." Margaret gave Buddy a warm kiss on the cheek as she walked him to the door. I heard him tell her how much he had enjoyed the evening, they exchanged a series of *bon soirs*, and *au revoirs*, and finally the door closed behind him.

When he was gone, and Margaret had drifted upstairs, smiling to herself, Cissy turned to me. "Raymio, I think they really like each other."

"That, dear heart," I said, pulling her close, "is the understatement of the year."

TEN

Early the next morning I phoned Hammett at home. "I'd like to go over the Enright case with you—to get your input. I've developed a theory that's pretty incredible."

"Okay," said Hammett. "Willie Hearst has invited me up to his ranch and Buddy's going to drive me. Why not come along? We can talk on the way. Ever been to Willie's joint?"

"No," I said, "but I've read a lot about the place."

"It's the cat's pajamas," declared Hammett. "Nothing else remotely like it."

"Okay," I said. "Shall I meet you?"

"No, we'll pick you up. By the way, Buddy tells me he had a great time last night. Talked about Proust and Faulkner. Hell, I didn't know he *read* Proust and Faulkner."

"There's a lot about Buddy you don't know."

"Yeah, I suppose. Well, just sit tight and we'll be right over. You might pack a toothbrush. If we're lucky, we'll be asked to spend the night."

"I'll be ready," I said.

I knew a bit about San Simeon ("Willie's joint"), located north of Santa Barbara in San Luis Obispo County. To use its

111

formal name, La Cuesta Encantada—The Enchanted Hill. Situated on a high knoll some two thousand feet above the Pacific, set against the Santa Lucia Mountains, and crowning a quarter million acres of privately owned land half the size of Rhode Island, San Simeon is a genuine world marvel.

Its owner, newspaper magnate William Randolph Hearst, insists on calling it "the ranch," and, indeed, some half a hundred cowhands are employed to deal with the herds of prime Jersey and Holstein cattle that roam its foothill ranges. There is also a fully functioning dairy farm.

San Simeon is huge, over a hundred-plus acres of palatial buildings, guesthouses, gardens, terraces, and pools, including the world's largest private zoo. I've talked with people who've been invited there, people in arts and politics mostly, and I've read several newspaper and magazine articles about it. The extraordinary details stand out in my mind.

The man who turned his dream of a hilltop castle into reality, the inimitable W. R. Hearst himself, reigns as a king in his own publishing domain (twenty-six major newspapers at last count, including two in L.A., the *Examiner* and the *Herald-Express*), backed up by a far-flung business complex of paper mills, mines, ranches, real-estate holdings, and warehouses jammed with global art treasures. Thousands of employees, over whom he rules with absolute authority, maintain his vast empire.

I looked forward to my impending visit with a keen sense of curiosity and anticipation.

"So . . . what do you think?" I asked. "Is it possible that Enright is DuPlaine's killer?"

We were in the backseat of Hammett's limousine, with Buddy driving us upcoast. I'd filled Dash in regarding my talk with McQuillan and my latest encounter with Carmilla at the Blue

Dove, and had just laid out my theory on Merv Enright's possible involvement in the DuPlaine murder.

Hammett sat back on the dark, wine-colored leather seat, lips pursed, considering my last question.

"Well," I repeated, "what do you think? Have I gone too far on this?"

Hammett tugged thoughtfully at his left earlobe. "Enright's an interesting suspect. He knew from Elina that the Countess depended emotionally on DuPlaine for her career, plus, according to Bobbie Haining, Merv considered the guy a phony."

"Of course, there's absolutely no proof that Enright was involved in DuPlaine's death," I pointed out.

"That doesn't mean the proof isn't there," said Hammett. "It just hasn't been *found* yet. When we locate Enright we may find the evidence we need to tie him to the murder."

I grinned at Hammett. "What's all this 'we' stuff? Don't you mean when *I* find Enright?"

"Oh, sure, that's what I mean."

And he grinned back at me.

I asked Hammett about his friendship with Hearst.

"We're not friends," he corrected me. "Willie just likes my writing. Three years ago he phoned his man at King Features and said he planned to launch a new comic strip for his papers and told him to get me to write it. Hearst was all worked up over *Dick Tracy* and *Dan Dunn, Secret Operative 48,* and wanted a strip that would combine the two, so I gave him *Secret Agent X-9.*"

"Big hit," I said. "Had you ever worked on a comic strip before?"

Hammett shook his head. "Never. But the money was just too good to turn down. So I said I'd do it. Ended up writing the dialogue and continuity on the first four X-9s." He chuckled. "I stole from myself—used plots from my old pulp stories. All crap, naturally, but it paid some bills."

"Why has Hearst invited you to San Simeon?"

"My guess is he wants to offer me more money for more crap. We'll find out. 'Come see me at the ranch,' he said, and so I'm on the way."

"And you're sure he won't object to my tagging along?"

"Naw. Willie's joint is always full of strangers. Dukes and earls and counts and mayors and presidents and movie stars and studio moguls. They come and go. Hell, he's got more than fifty guest bedrooms. Just remember to be nice to Marion and you'll fit right in."

"Marion Davies?"

"Well, he named one of his elephants Marion, but you don't have to be nice to the elephant. Yeah, I mean Davies, who is, by the way, a sweet number. Hotsy-totsy blonde. Not that she's a kid anymore. In her late thirties, but looks real good. Keeps herself up. I met her once."

"Isn't Hearst a lot older?"

"Yeah, a lot. Into his early seventies now. Still, with his dough, he could have any jane in America. But Lady Marion is all he wants. Worships her—and has since the day they met. I hear some guy kept putting the moves on her after Hearst warned him off, and the old boy had him iced. But that's probably just a rumor."

"Davies was a Follies girl, wasn't she?"

"In the beginning she was. With Ziegfeld. Hearst saw her when she was dancing in New York and got her into pictures. Assigned a full-time publicity man to cover her career, and had a fourteen-room bungalow built for her on the M-G-M lot. He personally supervises all her pictures."

"I saw one of them," I told him. "Something about the big top. It wasn't much good."

Hammett nodded. "That was *Polly of the Circus*. She's done a lot of empty-headed comedies. Stuff like *The Floradora Girl* and *Peg o' My Heart*. Hearst keeps pushing her for an Academy Award and she can barely talk. Stutters like crazy when she gets upset. At least she has a realistic view of her own ability. Says her career is five percent talent and ninety-five percent publicity. But with Daddy Hearst, she's got a good thing going and she knows it."

"I read somewhere that he designed San Simeon for her."

"When Hearst's mother died about fifteen years ago he inherited the property. Back then it was mostly undeveloped, just a few scattered ranch houses. He wanted a castle for his princess to live in, so he built a real lulu. And as soon as he found out that Marion liked animals he began putting his zoo together."

"What's he got in there?"

"Everything from lions and tigers to camels and kangaroos. Some in cages, with the rest running wild. Had to build a ten-mile fence to keep 'em inside."

"I've heard he owns some pretty exotic animals from around the world."

"Definitely," nodded Hammett. "He's got gorillas from Africa, spotted deer from India, sacred monkeys from Japan, yak from Tibet, and emu from Australia. Plus his horses—more than three dozen thoroughbred Arabians. That's because Marion likes to ride."

I settled back into the limo's soft leather seat, making the decision not to think about solving murders or finding lost sisters. Not for a while at least.

I was headed for La Cuesta Encantada—and I was ready for some enchantment.

From the main highway Buddy swung the big limo onto a six-mile private road that curved up past a lush profusion of trees and vegetation. The grade increased as we neared the summit.

"When the old man started building here," Hammett said, "the hilltop was practically bare. Now it's like a jungle—*his* jungle. Once, when he was in Paso Robles, he fancied a row of thirty-foot cypress trees, so he bought the whole row, had 'em boxed, and moved up here."

"He doesn't seem to care about how much he spends," I said.

"You don't know the half of it. Hearst travels to Europe every year searching for things to ship to the States. Buys entire Gothic rooms, carved ceilings, staircases, palace walls, stained glass windows, Greek columns. He owns sculpture going back four thousand years."

"My God! How much has all this cost?"

"Who knows? Willie spends money as fast as he makes it, and I've heard he takes in over fifteen million a year. You can do a lot with fifteen million a year."

"What kind of a man is he? I've heard a lot of stories about his being extremely rigid and conservative."

"Not always," grinned Hammett. "Ilka Chase told me that when she was a guest up here the old man goosed her in the Roman pool. He claimed he was just helping her out when his hand slipped."

As we crested the hill I got my first look at San Simeon. Detailed description is impossible; the "ranch" is simply too vast, too ornate, too extensive in scope and size for me to convey more than a hint of what I encountered.

Mainly, there are four palatial buildings of Spanish and Italian design—three massive guesthouses and a huge central structure of a hundred rooms known as La Casa Grande. This "big house," flanked by a pair of thrusting medieval towers, overlooks an immense outdoor "pool of Neptune." Scores of classic Greek and Roman sculptures, in Carrara marble, decorate the grounds. And when Hearst's guests prefer to avoid the sun, he provides them with a heated indoor pool in the style of an ancient Roman bath, elaborately tiled in shades of lapis lazuli and gold.

As Hammett had predicted, the place was swarming with celebrities and representatives of the world's power elite. I didn't recognize any of the politicians or members of European royalty, but I spotted Greta Garbo, Clark Gable, Gloria Swanson, and Jean Harlow, all of whom appeared to be having a dandy time.

"Willie keeps a tight rein on the booze," Hammett told me. "You won't see any drunks at San Simeon."

One of Hearst's butlers, a solemn, rail-thin fellow with a sallow complexion and a hushed voice, led us inside the main house to the master's lavish study.

Hearst seemed genuinely delighted to see Hammett, delivering a vigorous handshake and a wide smile. His voice was high and piping, and he sounded a lot like Mickey Mouse, yet he was an impressive man, radiating power and confidence, his pale eyes deeply set in a high-domed face. I'd heard that he enjoyed dressing casually, but I wasn't quite prepared for his garish red plaid sports jacket, kelly green shirt, golf slacks, and two-tone shoes.

Dash introduced me as a fellow writer, and Hearst firmly pumped my hand.

"I greatly admire individuals who live by their imagination," he said. "Yours is a rare and wondrous gift bestowed on but a select few. Your art harks back to ancient times—to the dawn of man, when we all gathered in caves to be entertained by storytellers."

"It's wonderful to meet someone who appreciates the storyteller's art," I said lamely, feeling at a loss for le mot juste.

"Come along, gentlemen," Hearst instructed. "We'll talk in the library."

We followed him down a grand hallway, past shining rows of knights in full armor, golden-hued Renaissance oil paintings, and richly woven Flemish tapestries, into the main library.

117

"The coffered Spanish ceiling dates from the sixteenth century," said Hearst.

He also pointed out his truly stunning collection of ancient Greek vases displayed on a plate rail above glassed wall cases containing thousands of rare books.

Indicating a tall blue-and-gold vase with a frieze of painted figures encircling it, he noted: "Fourth century B.C. A favorite of mine. Apulian volute-handled krater. Very difficult to come by."

"I'll bet," I said, with genuine respect. Another lame reply. Talking to this man was not easy.

He walked over to a painting in a corner alcove—of a woman, a member of some royal European family, with a small, furry creature in her lap.

"That's a ferret she's holding," said Hearst.

"What's she doing with a rodent in her lap?" asked Hammett.

Hearst chuckled. "Back in the Middle Ages, when this picture was painted, people never bathed. As a result, they became infested with body lice and other unpleasant vermin. So the upper classes carried personal ferrets with them; the animals would spend their days crawling around their owners, feasting off the bounty of their bodies. If you happened to be a ferret, it was a very good life."

"Yeck!" I said, with a shiver.

"Ditto," said Hammett.

"Allow me to show you something else you might find intriguing," said Hearst. He moved to an intricately carved, lacquered Chinese cabinet near the window and unlocked it with a tiny gold key. The inside drawers were lined with ornate vermeil plates, gold on exquisitely crafted silver, each nestled individually in red velvet. In the rainbowed sunlight from the stained glass window they glittered like a constellation of jewels.

"These originally came from a castle in the Bavarian Alps," he declared. "Charles the First owned them in 1645. Quite lovely, don't you agree?"

"Quite," said Hammett.

As Hearst turned away to relock the cabinet, Dash nodded, snapping his fingers. "Bingo! The motive!"

"Huh?" I blinked at him.

"Didn't DuPlaine's killer make off with some valuable silver that night?"

I nodded. "The police report I saw itemized several trophies and bowls, plus a complete dinner set."

"Well, there you are," said Hammett. "We know Enright needed money. The silver would bring him instant cash. Motive for putting away DuPlaine."

"What are you talking about?" asked Hearst.

"Murder," said Hammett. "We were talking about David DuPlaine. You must have known him."

"Oh, quite well," nodded Hearst. "He stayed here at the ranch several times. It's always such a shock when someone you know personally becomes the victim of a violent crime." Hearst turned and took his place at the head of a massive Benedictine table.

We were about to sit down when Marion Davies walked in to join us. A striking beauty, with a direct, clear-eyed gaze and delicate porcelain features, she wore white boots, a fringed white buckskin riding skirt, and a matching vest. Her blonde hair was tied back with a blue grosgrain ribbon.

She rushed over to Hearst, kissing him on the cheek. "I took out Bounty Boy," she told him. "He's a *splendid* jumper."

Hearst looked worried. "Didn't I tell you not to go jumping walls and fences on that horse? You could take a terrible spill . . . break a leg or an arm. It's far too dangerous."

She laughed his warning away and turned to greet Dash. "I

remember you! You're Mr. Hammett." She swept her gaze to me. "But who's this?"

"Raymond Chandler." I smiled.

"Ray's an ace writer," declared Dash. "In *Black Mask*."

"Oh!" Marion beamed at me. "If you wear a black mask you must adore costume parties. We're always having them here at the ranch."

"I don't *wear* a black mask, I write for one. It's a crime-fiction magazine. I do stories for it."

"I see," nodded Marion, looking somewhat disappointed.

Hearst rubbed his hands together. "Well, let us all be seated and get down to business."

The word set off Marion. "I *hate* business!" she declared, beginning to stutter. "B-b-business, b-b-business, b-business! I just want to have *fun*."

"But this is about you, pumpkin," said Hearst. "Please . . . sit down and listen."

"Oh, all right." She sat down next to Hearst.

He leaned across the table toward Hammett. "Now, Dash, I brought you up here for a very important reason. Marion is a supremely talented actress, but her range has yet to be properly explored. She has a tremendous potential that has not as yet been tapped." He leaned closer. "Marion is like a volcano waiting to erupt."

I thought this was a little strong, and I noticed that Hammett was trying hard to suppress a smile, but Hearst went on to amplify his point.

"Yours is a literary talent of rare power," he told Hammett. "I want to harness that power, put it to work for us. I want a picture that will rock the industry, that will guarantee her an Oscar, a starring vehicle for Marion Davies that only you can write."

"Well, I—" began Hammett, but Hearst cut him off, fire in his eyes.

"Something fresh and bold—but not vulgar. The film audience detests vulgarity, you know. I was thinking of a picture with the sweeping emotional power of *Ramona* . . . perhaps we could set it in Old Mexico instead of California. A tender romance in which Marion finds her spiritual awakening in the arms of a brave and dashing cavalier. I was thinking, perhaps we could set it in the time of the French occupation of Mexico, when Maximilian and Carlota were monarchs. That way we could have the romance of Old Mexico *combined* with the glittering sophistication of Europe."

"Oh, that *would* be fun," enthused Marion.

Hammett smiled. "Selznik just did one like that on the desert," he said. "Dietrich and Boyer in *The Garden of Allah*."

"Hmmm . . ." Hearst frowned and stroked his chin, thinking. Then he looked up in triumph.

"I have it!" he said, standing up from the table. "France! Of course . . . Joan of Arc! An instantly recognizable role with *depth*. A guaranteed contender for an Academy Award."

"It's been done," said Hammett, "three or four times already. *Joan the Woman* in 1916, *The Passion of Joan of Arc* in 1928, and *St. Joan the Maid* in 1930. I think they even did a version in Germany last year."

I marveled at Hammett's grasp of film lore; he not only worked in the industry, he knew its detailed history.

Hearst was not discouraged. "My version will be different," he declared. "To give it some zip during these dark economic times, we'll do it as a *musical!* Musicals are always successful at the box office. Whenever Louis B. Mayer loses money on an 'art' film, he makes another musical."

Hammett was shaking his head. "I don't think I can—"

"Of *course* you can!" Hearst cut in. "I'll pay you fifty thousand to write it—and I'll send you to France with a suite at the finest hotel in Paris."

"I can use the fifty gees okay," said Hammett. "And the trip would be nice. But I just don't do musical religious biographies."

Hearst frowned, sat down again, and tented his fingers. "Unfortunate. Most unfortunate. The more I think about this Joan of Arc idea the more I'm excited by it. A complete change of pace. Religion with a joyous musical spirit to uplift the downtrodden masses." He shifted his pale eyes to me. "How about you, Mr. Chandler? Could *you* write the role of a lifetime for my Marion?"

"I'm sorry, sir. I don't work in pictures," I said.

Hearst stood up with a heavy sigh and reached for Marion's hand. "Come, my dove, the King of Siam is waiting for us in the billiard room." He bowed to us from the door. "I bid you good day, gentlemen. The butler will show you out."

We stood silently on the thick Renaissance rug after Hearst and Marion Davies had gone. Hammett looked dazed.

"You just kissed fifty thousand bucks good-bye," I said.

"Yeah, I know," muttered Hammett. "Plus a free trip to France." He chuckled. "Must be my big year for musicals. That guy Welles wanted to make one out of *The Dain Curse*."

"Maybe you should have taken a crack at Hearst's idea," I said.

"Not really. I've heard too many horror stories from other writers about what it's like working for Willie on a Davies picture. It's sheer hell, Ray."

"Then why come all the way up here if you don't want to work for him?"

"I was hoping he'd ask me to adapt one of my own stories for the good Lady Marion. Something like 'The Girl With the Silver Eyes' or 'The Big Knockover.' That I could possibly have handled."

"He seemed really upset," I said. "Didn't even ask us to spend the night. I was looking forward to telling Cissy about a sumptuous castle dinner and a bedroom of royal splendor."

Hammett shrugged. "He should get Ben Hecht to do his damn musical. Ben can write anything."

Which is when the sallow-faced butler appeared to lead us out of the castle.

It had been a most interesting afternoon.

ELEVEN

Some intense research on the Countess was paying off for me. Despite the lack of mention in her official studio biographies, I discovered an article in the society section of the *Examiner*, complete with white-tie photo, which revealed that about seven years before, Carmilla had been married to a small-time silent-screen actor named Jack Snowden, who had, by that time, retired from show business and gone into real estate. Further research revealed that he had been much more successful in his new occupation and had somehow ended up with a flock of fancy apartment buildings on Wilshire.

I thought it might be a good idea to talk to Snowden. Not that I expected him to know anything about Merv Enright, but he might be able to fill me in on more of Carmilla's past. I wondered why she hadn't told me about him. Maybe he knew things she didn't want *me* to know. Or maybe he just didn't seem important enough to mention in regard to her missing sister.

But I was curious, nonetheless.

Jack Snowden's number was in the phone book so I had no trouble making contact with him. I fudged on the reason, telling Snowden that I was writing an article for one of the film magazines on Carmilla's early life, and would he be willing to talk to me about her?

We agreed to meet at his home on Angelo Drive in Benedict Canyon. He was giving a birthday party for Carol, his five-year-old daughter, and would be showing some Disney cartoons for the kids. We could talk while the cartoons were screening. Fine. I drove over that same afternoon.

Snowden's estate testified to his business acumen; I was waved through a tall ornamental iron gate, initialed with a large S in bronze, onto a curving burgundy-brick drive leading to a white, three-story Moorish mansion shaded by acacia trees. The hedges were all neatly trimmed and everything sparkled; a weed wouldn't dare show up in these well-groomed surroundings. I drove past the main house into a large cobblestoned rear courtyard already jammed with guest cars.

A smartly uniformed attendant was there to park my Duesenberg. "Mr. Snowden is with the children on the south lawn," he told me when I handed him the keys.

Leaving the courtyard, I walked down a gravel path lined with pink and white geraniums, passing under a spreading arbor of red roses to the main party area.

A large, candy-striped tent had been erected on the wide manicured lawn, while a calliope-accompanied merry-go-round revolved next to it, each seat occupied by a squealing boy or girl. A painted clown, in baggy polka dots, was performing magic tricks in front of the tent for a dozen wide-eyed children while their beaming parents stood by, observing the act and sipping cocktails.

Uniformed servants moved among the adult guests with drinks and hors d'oeuvres. I asked one of the waiters about Jack Snowden. "I believe you'll find Mr. Snowden inside the tent, sir, with Miss Carol."

Under the canvas an impressive array of fruit, salads, finger sandwiches, ice cream, and decorated petits fours covered a long, linen-draped table which reminded me nostalgically of English high tea. The tent was crowded with guests, each of the children wearing a colorful crepe paper hat. Everyone was chomping happily away.

I had no trouble spotting Snowden, who looked to be a slightly older version of his news photo. He was standing at the table's far end, spooning cut fruit and orange gelatin onto plates for two frothily dressed children. Balding slightly, with an Errol Flynn mustache, he was tall and tanned in a white knit pullover and tennis slacks.

"I'm Chandler," I said.

He wiped his fingers on a damask napkin before shaking hands. "This is Carol, my baby birthday girl."

"I'm not a baby anymore, Daddy," she said with some indignation. "I'm *five!*" Then she turned to me and gave a little curtsy. "Pleased to meet you, Mr. Chandler."

Snowden beamed at her perfect manners.

I smiled down at the child. She was dressed like a fairy princess in a white lace dress decorated with seed pearls and pink satin roses. "Hello, Carol," I said. "Happy birthday."

"Thank you!" She glanced to the girl at her side. "I'd like you to meet Shirley, my very best friend."

The curly-haired youngster standing beside Carol looked up from her plate of jiggling salad. She was Shirley Temple.

"It's very nice meeting you, sir," she said, smiling that dimpled, world-famous smile.

Snowden was amused by my flustered reaction. In my mind, I was at sixes and sevens; what *does* one say to an eight-year-old global phenomenon?

"My wife and I saw you in *The Little Colonel*," I said. "We thought you did a fine job. Especially the stairway dance—that was our favorite part of the picture."

126

"Oh, with Mr. Robinson," Shirley said brightly. "He's a wonderful man; I just *loved* working with him. He makes everything fun."

Snowden looked at his wristwatch. "Why don't you girls run along now. Mr. Chandler and I have to talk."

"Bye, bye, Mr. Chandler," said Carol.

"I'm real happy to have met you," said Shirley.

I watched the two little Hollywood princesses walk away together hand in hand.

A perfect scene. Even Dash Hammett couldn't have written it any better.

Snowden's den was located in the west wing. Antique windows faced a traditional Spanish patio that looked as if it could have belonged to El Cid. A blue-tiled water fountain in the center of the garden sparkled with golden light from the afternoon sun. Palm trees shaded smooth stone paths bordered with a profusion of jasmine, hibiscus, and gardenias. Through the open windows I inhaled the rich, sweet smell of tropical blossoms.

The den was furnished in the luxuriously spare style of Spain's El Escorial castle: leather-topped desk, leather couch and armchairs, even leather-framed portraits on the wall—of his current wife and of Carol. Obviously, Jack Snowden was partial to leather. There was nothing in the room to suggest that he'd ever been married to Carmilla Blastok.

"My wife, Nancy, is in New York," he was telling me. "She was desperate to be here for Carol's birthday, but she had to be at the industry showings of next winter's line. Has her own company. Designs children's clothing. Too much lace and velvet for my taste, but the Whitneys and Rockefellers think she's wonderful." He grinned. "If your son needs a Little Lord Fauntleroy suit for cotillion, or your daughter needs a Belgian lace dress for afternoon tea, I can get you a real good deal."

I smiled. "Thanks, but we just have a cat, and she prefers her own fur." I looked around the impressive room. "So you and your wife have both been successful," I said.

"I credit Nan with my success. She's a vibrant, energetic, ambitious woman. Keeps me on my toes. I'm the kind of guy who needs pushing. Nan's a great pusher."

"As they say, a strong woman behind every strong man."

"Excuse me, I'm forgetting my manners. Would you like a drink, Mr. Chandler?"

"No, I'm fine, thank you."

He crossed his long legs on the couch. "Well, then . . . let's talk about Carmilla. What is it you'd like to know?"

"Tell me about your marriage."

"It only lasted two years," declared Snowden, rubbing the bridge of his nose. "I had a bit part in one of her Dragon films. Rich playboy who falls under the Dragon's deadly spell. I ended on the rack in her underground torture chamber." He smiled. "We played it for ham in those days. Eye-rolling, arm-waving melodrama. The silents weren't very subtle. I remember Buster Keaton used to come over to the set all the time to watch Carmilla. Had a real crush on her."

"Did you and Carmilla fall in love during the picture?"

"Well, I suppose you could say that. It was pretty elemental. We were all over each other from the first day of shooting. She's a very intense woman, sexually. A real animal. Or, at least, that's how she *used* to be, when I knew her. I don't know what she's like now."

"How long before the two of you married?"

"Six months. She wanted the marriage and kept putting pressure on me. I had strong doubts. I didn't think marrying her was such a keen idea."

"Why?"

"Because I knew that Carmilla was incapable of being faithful to me."

"And were you right?"

He nodded. "She had at least three affairs during our marriage. I put up with the first two because I knew she wasn't serious about them. But the thing with DuPlaine . . . as far as I was concerned, *that* one did it."

I stared at him. "But I understood that there was nothing sexual between David DuPlaine and Carmilla."

"Are you kidding?" He got up from the leather couch, walked to a carved Castilian chest, and raised the lid. He rummaged around, then took out a white envelope and handed it to me. "Have a look."

I opened the envelope and removed a photo of DuPlaine and Carmilla, naked, locked together in a passionate embrace.

"I found them in our bed," said Snowden. "They didn't hear me come in. I decided to get my Kodak and record the moment for posterity. Makes a nice keepsake. When the judge saw it, I had no trouble getting a divorce."

I gave the photo back to him and he replaced it in the chest.

"She told me that DuPlaine was her creative mentor," I said. "She made their relationship sound almost spiritual."

"That's partially true," said Snowden, sitting down again in one of the leather chairs. "He *did* reshape Carmilla's career when sound came along. I don't know what she would have done without him. He got her into all those vampire pictures, the ones that made her famous. But basically, they just liked to screw."

"What about his death?" I asked. "Do you accept the story that he was killed by a burglar?"

"Why not? I have no reason to believe anyone else was responsible. I know that Carmilla was shattered, personally as well as professionally. It destroyed her. She gave up films after that."

"I think I know who killed him," I said.

His eyebrows arched. "Who?"

"I don't want to say until I have proof. Right now, I'm working from a hunch."

"Is there anything else I can help you with?"

"What can you tell me about Carmilla's sister?"

"Elly? She was still a kid when Carmilla and I got divorced. She did pictures for a while, but I haven't heard anything about her in years."

"Well, thanks for your time."

Snowden stood up, indicating our meeting had come to an end. "I hope I've been of some assistance to you in writing your piece." Then he chuckled. "Actually, no film magazine is going to print what I told you about Carmilla."

"I suppose not," I said. "It doesn't matter. I'll just stick with her early films and leave you out of it. But I do value your frankness."

"It's a strange thing to admit," said Snowden as he walked me down a long hall to the front door, "but I grew to love Carmilla. Not that I trusted her, and I certainly didn't want to stay married to her. But . . . somehow . . . despite everything, I loved her. When we finally broke up, it hurt. Had to happen, but it hurt anyway. That make any sense to you?"

"Makes a lot of sense," I told him. "When people fall in love, it isn't always logical—it just happens."

"I'm glad you understand," he said. "I felt like a fool, loving Carmilla. It seemed . . . almost perverted."

"But you're over it now."

"Yes, thank God. I have a wonderful wife and child, and an active career. Those early days are no more than a dream. Unreal, like smoke. I seldom think about Carmilla anymore . . . usually only when a magazine story or something brings her to mind."

Walking back to my Duesenberg I had a whole new perspective on the Countess.

No wonder she hadn't mentioned Jack Snowden!

TWELVE

On the way home to Culver City that afternoon I realized that another vehicle had been following me since I'd left Benedict Canyon. A rusted tan Ford truck with three men inside. They stayed about two cars back, steadily pacing me.

Maybe I was being paranoid. It was possible that these men just happened to be traveling in my direction. It didn't make any sense that someone would be tailing me.

I was on Venice Boulevard, nearing Metro-Goldwyn-Mayer, with the Ford a quarter block behind, when I decided to risk a traffic ticket by running a red light. If I was actually being followed, the Ford would also have to run the light to keep me in sight.

At the next corner, as the light blinked crimson, I gunned the Duesenberg, checking cross traffic to make sure I'd have a clear run through the intersection. It was safe and I shot across, still accelerating. In my driving mirror I saw the tan truck swerve around a braking Packard and zoom through the red. Horns blared in angry protest.

Who *were* these people, and why were they following my car?

Had they mistaken me for someone else? My knuckles whitened as I gripped the steering wheel. Breathing fast, sweat beginning to bead my forehead, I scanned both sides of Venice Boulevard for a police car. Nothing. At this moment I would have *welcomed* a traffic ticket.

Question: How to lose the Ford?

I had a half block on my pursuer when I swung hard right onto Motor Avenue and almost immediately took another tire-screaming left turn into a wide parking lot behind the Isis movie theater. I hoped the other driver would breeze on past without realizing where I'd gone.

No such luck. I'd left a trail of burned rubber on the street and the Ford's driver followed my tire tracks, roaring into the lot. The truck juddered to a stop just behind me. It was Sunday afternoon, with the theater closed, and the lot was deserted. I was isolated and vulnerable.

My scalp prickled; this was big trouble.

Both doors popped open on the truck cab and the men jumped out, walking purposefully toward me over the dark expanse of asphalt, the driver leading.

I got out to confront them, playing it moment by moment, a knot of fear tightening my stomach; I didn't know what to expect, but I had a strong feeling it wouldn't be pleasant.

The driver's face was shaded by a long-billed red and black plaid hunting cap. He was in torn dungarees and a badly scuffed leather jacket with a missing pocket. As he drew closer the slanting rays of the sun revealed his identity: the man in the photo with Elina. The same thick dark hair, narrow face, tight mouth—and the same eyes, like the eyes of a fox.

"Enright!"

His lip curled in an ugly sneer. "So you recognize me, huh? I thought maybe you would."

"How did you know that I—"

"That you were looking for me" he cut in. "Because Bobbie told me, that's how."

"Bobbie Haining?" I was genuinely confused. "But she said she had no idea what had happened to you."

"She lied. Me and Bobbie, we had a big thing going for a while there. After we broke it off, I left her a number to call in case she ever needed to reach me. She phoned to say you were nosing around. Told me your name—but it took me a while to run you down." His fox eyes narrowed into slits. "Who sent you after me . . . the Blastok bitch?"

"She wants to know that her sister is okay—that Elina is safe."

"I'll *bet* she does," Enright said. He glared at me. "I don't like anybody poking his nose into my life."

"Is Elina still with you?"

"None of your damn business!"

"I'd like to talk to you about her."

"We're not here to talk—*are* we, boys?"

I focused on the two men standing just behind Enright. Unshaven bruisers. The taller guy was over six feet, with shiny, slicked-down hair. His weathered skin was taut and leathery; you could bind books with it. The second bruiser was an inch or two shorter, but much wider—like a squared-off block of concrete. His hair was short and matted, and he had the flattened nose and cauliflower ears of a boxer. Snake-dark eyes were partially hidden by a thrusting ledge of bony forehead.

Enright stepped aside and his two muscle boys glided toward me, both sporting tight-lipped smiles that told me they enjoyed this sort of exercise.

"My friends are gonna make you real sorry you came looking for me" said Enright. He was smirking like a schoolyard bully.

"I'm sorry already," I said, backing toward the Duesenberg.

I thought of jumping inside and trying for a getaway, but such a move was impossible. No time. I didn't have a weapon of any kind with which to defend myself, and I knew I could never out-run them. Which meant I was due to take a savage beating. I was no pulp-story hero with an iron skull; I'd likely end up with several broken bones. A truly terrifying prospect.

Or maybe they'd kill me.

The tall one buried his right fist in my stomach and I doubled over, gasping for air. Gagging, I fell back against the Duesenberg's front fender—only to have my head snapped back by a stunning blow to the chin.

Dimly, I heard Enright's voice. "Al, you step back. Use the sap on him, Arnie."

Through pain-blurred eyes I saw the shorter man (Arnie) pull a nasty-looking blackjack from his coat pocket. But before he could use it the sound of a roaring engine filled the air and a long black limousine skidded to a stop between my car and the Ford truck.

Hammett leaned from the rear passenger window, a double-cocked 12-gauge sawed-off leveled across the door.

His face was twisted with anger, his tone as sharp as a woodsman's ax. "Back off, you frigging bastards, or I'll blow your guts all over the lot!"

His colorful warning caught their attention, but it was the shotgun that did the trick; no one argues with a loaded sawed-off. Enright's muscle boys edged back, eyes bugging, hands in the air. Merv, ghost white, also had both hands raised. "Easy does it, pal," he said softly.

I could see Buddy smiling behind the wheel, amused by Hammett's sudden effect on the trio. I had no doubt that Buddy would have waded into them on my behalf, but no such action was needed. Dash had the situation well under control.

"Climb in that damn truck of yours," he snapped, "and get lost. *Now!*"

135

They did that, piling awkwardly into the Ford's cab. Enright gunned the engine, accelerating rapidly out of the lot.

Hammett stepped from the limo and walked over to me. "You okay?"

"A little punchy, but I'll live," I said. "Where'd you get the shotgun?"

"I keep it stowed under the backseat," Hammett told me. "For emergencies." He grinned. "I figured this was a good time to bring it out."

I eased a slow hand along my jaw; the area was quite tender, but at least the bone hadn't been broken. And I still had all my teeth.

By now Buddy was standing next to me, asking if I'd been badly hurt. I told him no. "They were just getting started," I said. "If you guys hadn't come along when you did . . ."

Buddy smiled, a twinkle in his dark eyes. "You're wondering how we arrived like the Two Musketeers, *n'est pas?*"

"I never question Providence," I said, "but, in this case, I'll make an exception. *Tell* me!"

"I wanted to find out what happened with Jack Snowden," declared Hammett. (I'd informed him I was going to see Carmilla's ex-husband.) "When I phoned your house, Cissy said you hadn't returned yet, so I decided to have Buddy drive me over. We were almost to M-G-M when I saw you plow through that red light on Venice. Obviously, you were in some kind of trouble."

"That's when we spotted the truck," added Buddy. "We saw you turn fast onto Motor Avenue, and so we went after you."

Hammett nodded. "We passed the theater in our first run-by, but when we went back Buddy spotted your tire tracks leading into the lot, and there you were, getting the crap knocked out of you." He frowned. "Who *are* those guys?"

"The one in the leather jacket is Merv Enright."

"You found him!"

"No. He found *me*." I sighed. "That ex-girlfriend of yours in Rialto put him on my tail. She *had* been involved with him, after all. It appears that your Bobbie is a liar."

Hammett shrugged. "It figures. She's an actress, so she put on an act for us."

"The trouble is," I said, "I'm right back where I began. I don't know Enright's address, or if Elina is still with him."

"The girl might have his address," said Buddy.

"Doubt it," I said. "He gave her an emergency phone number, but that's likely all she's got. Besides, even if she does know where Enright is, she's not about to tell us. And we can't very well beat it out of her."

"We won't need to," said Hammett. His lean face wore a cunning half smile.

"You've got something!" I glared at him. "Don't play around with me, Dash. What have you got?"

"His license number," said Hammett.

"My God! I never thought to—"

"Here," he said, jotting down the number and handing it to me. "Put your Homicide pal McQuillan on it. He should be able to dig up an address."

"Will do," I said. Then I hesitated, looking intently at Hammett. "There's one thing I have to know."

"What's that?"

"The threat you made . . . about blowing their guts out. Would you have done it? Would you have actually *killed* them?"

"I don't make a habit of killing people," said Hammett. "For all I knew, those three guys could have been cops." He grinned. "I mean, you *did* run a red light."

"That's a relief to hear," I told him. "I thought you meant it."

"Which was exactly the impression I wanted to convey," he said. "But even if I'd pulled the triggers, those mugs would still be alive."

"I don't—"

"The sawed-off isn't loaded," Hammett declared. "I keep it for *effect*. I've never carried shells for it. We just managed to pull off what's known as an empty bluff."

"Which worked beautifully," I said.

"Yeah," Dash nodded. "If it hadn't, we'd *all* be going to the hospital."

Cissy and Margaret hovered over me that evening like a pair of Florence Nightingales. Was I feeling dizzy? Nauseous? Did my head ache? Shouldn't I see a doctor? No, no, no. And no. I finally convinced them that I was fine. Just a sore jaw . . . and a few purple bruises which Margaret insisted on treating with her "Great-granny's no-fail old-timey remedy": a poultice of grated uncooked turnip. It actually *did* seem to help.

"Those dreadful men belong behind bars!" Cissy declared.

"You should report this to the police and press assault charges," said Margaret.

"I just need to find Merv Enright—and Elina," I said.

"You could be attacked again!" Cissy declared. "That Enright is a public menace!"

"Remember how all this started?" I said. "You asked me to find out why and how Julian died. I'm still trying to do that. Elina had a relationship with him. Once I find her, she may be able to tell me things. And I think she's still with Merv Enright. I'm gambling on that."

"Just don't gamble your *life* on it," said Margaret.

She had a point.

THIRTEEN

By noon the following day, McQuillan had come through. He supplied an address for Enright.

"You're a peach," I told him. "Thank God for honest cops."

"Keep me in the picture," Art said. "I want to know what happens when you find this guy. If you *do* manage to uncover anything that ties him to the DuPlaine killing, I need to know about it, pronto."

"Pronto," I said, and expressed my gratitude for his help.

Next I phoned Hammett, telling him that I was headed for the Grandview Apartments in Hollywood, on Wilcox, and did he want to meet me there?

"Damn right I do," he said. "Whoever arrives first waits for the other."

"Okay," I said.

The trip from Culver City took about forty minutes and when I got there I found Hammett's limo parked under a drooping pepper tree on Wilcox. It was hot, with the intense Southern California sun baking the streets, so I left my coat in the Duesenberg. Hammett said something to Buddy, got out, and we walked to the Grandview—which was anything but grand. A sagging,

down-at-the-heels wooden structure of indeterminate color—
something between dirt brown and soot gray—it perched behind
a mass of untrimmed devil grass and yellow wild mustard
flowers.

The interior wasn't any grander. We walked across a cracked
linoleum floor to a grizzled old party bent over a grimed reception desk. There was a calendar on the wall behind the desk featuring a buxom young miss in a knit swimsuit. She looked fine,
but the calendar was a year out of date.

Pop wore a pair of bifocals that rode halfway down his mot-
tled nose; his hairless skull gleamed like a polished egg and he
hadn't cleaned his fingernails since Teddy Roosevelt climbed
San Juan Hill.

"Whatcha fellas want?" Before we could tell him, he wagged a
bony finger at us. "If yer lookin' to rent, we ain't got no rooms.
Full up, we are."

"That's a real disappointment," said Hammett. "I was planning to spend my honeymoon here."

"We've been told that a Merv Enright lives at this address," I
said. "We'd like to see him."

"Can't."

"Why not?"

"Ain't here."

"You mean, he's out?"

"Gone. Moved."

"Where?"

"I don't have no exact address," said the old geezer. "Had to
send somethin' of his over to a trailer park in Venice, but I don't
recollect when. Long time ago."

"*How* long?"

He corkscrewed an index finger into his left ear, then studied
the waxy residue at the tip of his finger with the concentration of
a pawn broker examining a cheap pocket watch. Finally, he swung

140

up his bald head and answered me: "Year. Maybe longer."

"When he was here, did a woman named Elina Knibbs live in the apartment with him?" asked Hammett.

"Don't recollect."

I pressed the issue. "We're not here to cause trouble for you, but we *do* need to know. He *was* living with a woman, wasn't he?"

The old man was hesitant, fearing the possible consequences of allowing illegal cohabitation in his establishment.

"Coulda been. I don't pay no mind to dirty gossip. Long as people keep the rent up is all that matters."

"Do you have Enright's Venice address in your files?" asked Hammett.

The wiry white brows went up. *"Files?* Don't keep no files. Never have. Never will."

"And you don't recall the address?"

"I *said* that, didn't I?" The old geezer scowled. "Man can't be expected to remember every damn thing in the whole wide world!"

"Fine," I said. "We appreciate your cooperation."

Dash and I walked back across the cracked linoleum, but just before we exited the old man yelled after us: "Never liked that son of a bitch! Had a real unfriendly kinda character."

I turned to him, rubbing a hand along my bruised jaw. "I know what you mean. Might even call him nasty."

"Yup," nodded the oldster. "That's it exact. *Nasty.* A nasty one, he was."

Hammett and I walked out the door.

There couldn't be many trailer parks in Venice. Therefore, at this point, I told myself that finding Merv Enright shouldn't be all that difficult.

Unless he'd moved again.

We'd find out soon enough.

Caution was the order of the day. If we managed to locate Enright in Venice, we had to make sure we didn't panic him. He
must remain unaware that he'd been tracked down. Otherwise,
our pigeon would once again be on the wing. Which meant that
Enright must be approached by someone he wouldn't recognize.
He knew me all too well, and he would never forget the man
behind that leveled sawed-off. Hammett and I, therefore, had to
stay clear of him.

Yet we needed to move fast. If this man was a killer, as I
strongly suspected, then Elina remained in continual danger. Enright could turn on her at any moment; his behavior in attacking
me had clearly demonstrated his violent nature. Carmilla was
correct in expressing worry about her sister. Then again, perhaps
Elina had left him. Until we found Enright, we couldn't be sure
of anything.

Hammett sent Buddy home with the limo and accompanied
me as I drove to Gardner's place in the Hollywood hills. By now,
I hoped, Erle would be back from his desert outing.

He was. We found him in the greenhouse behind his garage,
watering some pink Amazonian orchids. I've never liked orchids. They remind me of dead flesh. When I explained the situation, Erle put the watering can aside, told Tomas not to expect
him back until much later, and quickly changed clothes. He
climbed into the Duesenberg next to Hammett and we were off.

"So I'm your front man," Gardner said.

"He's never seen you," I told him. "If we find Enright's
trailer, you do the talking to him. The main thing we need to
know right now is whether or not Elina Knibbs is still with him."

Erle regarded the purple bruise on my jaw. "Really socked
you, huh?"

"He had his mugs work me over. They might have killed me if

Dash hadn't shown up. Enright's a tough customer."

"If Elina Knibbs *is* there, what do I say to her?"

"Nothing. I'll need to get her alone to question her. That will come later."

The early history of Venice, California, has always intrigued me.

Shortly after the turn of the century, the first of the wealthy cigarette kings, Abbot Kinney, purchased a large tract of Southern California marshland near the Pacific Ocean where, in 1905, he proceeded to build an American version of the famous canal city of Italy. He called it "Venice-by-the-Sea" and it was designed to function as a center of social elegance and high culture.

In the beginning, the city lived up to its promise. Californians were serenaded by authentically costumed gondoliers as they boated down an array of glittering canals. Ornate hotels lined the beach and a new amusement park provided thrills for thousands of visitors. In a triumph for culture, the legendary actress Sarah Bernhardt was lured there to perform *Camille.*

Gradually, however, the canals became polluted due to poor engineering design; they were eventually condemned as a public health menace. By 1925, most of them had been filled in and the gondolas were in dry rot. A forest of ungainly oil derricks had sprouted along Venice streets, killing the last vestige of scenic charm. Now, more than a decade later, the ill-fated city retained nothing of its former beauty. It was just another sand-blown, sunfaded California beach town.

The phone book listed three trailer parks in the area. We checked out the first two without success. When we questioned their owners, showing Enright's photograph, they assured us that he'd never rented space from them. They had never seen the man.

Our last stop was the Crescent Moon Trailer Court, a block

off Venice Boulevard just short of the beach.

"I've got a hunch this is the one," I told Hammett and Gardner.

"If you're right, and we find him," said Erle, "you don't think he'll turn violent on me, do you?"

I shook my head. "Not if you don't provoke him. We just need to make sure he's living at this place, and if Elina is with him."

"Since Enright doesn't know you," said Hammett, "there's no reason for him to give you any trouble."

"Okay," said Gardner. "Actually, it should be kind of fun."

I parked the Duesenberg in an alley between two buildings a block from the trailer park. If Enright was in the vicinity, I wanted to make sure he didn't spot the car.

We walked over to the Crescent Moon Trailer Court. It lacked a crescent moon. A tall wooden sign bore the court's name in scrolled red letters, but the painter had neglected to put in the moon. Or maybe nobody gave a damn.

It had that look—of nobody giving a damn. The lot had never been properly graded; of rutted dirt and sand, and choked with patches of scraggly weed, it was surrounded by an unpainted wooden fence, many of the slats missing, and a row of unkempt eucalyptus trees. Two dozen dented trailers were parked on the lot, like derelict ships washed ashore. Every space sported its own unpainted wooden utility shed and its own set of sagging clotheslines; pegged laundry provided an intimate look into the dreary lives of the park's occupants.

At the street entrance to the park a small corrugated metal shack was marked OFFICE in sputtering neon. Whoever owned the place obviously kept it lit all day. The first three letters had blackened; by night the message it conveyed would be confusing.

We sent Gardner in to inquire about Enright while we waited in the cool shadow of the building.

144

"I think Erle figures this as a lark," declared Hammett.

"Well, *he* didn't get punched in the stomach," I said. "Me, I take Mr. Enright very seriously."

After a few moments Erle came out of the office, nodding to us. "Our boy's here all right," he said. "Trailer five." He pointed. "The red one close to the fence, underneath the tree."

"Great," I said. "Did you find out if anyone else is living with him?"

"Nope," said Erle. "I didn't want to seem too nosy. I just asked about Enright."

"Got your cover story all worked out?" I asked.

"To perfection," he said.

In place of his usual sports outfit, Erle had changed into a suit, tie, and vest before we left his house, in keeping with his intended role as a salesman. His leather briefcase and wire-rimmed glasses completed the image.

"Don't say anything to rouse his suspicion," I warned Erle. "If he answers your knock and nobody is standing behind him, see if you can coax Elina to the door. Providing she's there, of course. If she is, maybe *she'll* answer."

"All this jabber is useless," Hammett complained sourly. "Erle knows what to do. Let him *do* it."

"I guess I'm a little nervous," I admitted.

"Go on, Erle," said Hammett. "We'll be watching from the fence. Now, scat!"

As Gardner walked toward the red trailer, I sighed. "Let's hope he's home."

"He is," said Hammett. "I can see the nose of his truck in back of the trailer."

At the fence, I pressed close to the rough-grained wood, peering through a gap where three slats were missing. From this vantage point, underneath the leafy branches of the eucalyptus tree, we could see and hear everything.

Erle reached the trailer and mounted the steps leading to the door. He knocked. Waited. Knocked again.

A bumping sound came from within. Then the door swung open and Merv Enright was there, in rumpled pants and a torn undershirt, looking mean. He needed a shave, a haircut, and a new personality.

"Yeah?" he growled. "What the hell do *you* want?"

"I'm Hiram Bixby," Erle told him brightly. "Bixby Life . . . the insurance policy that leaves you with an inner glow of security. This week we happen to have a special on—"

"Breeze!" snapped Enright. "I don't need no friggin' insurance."

Then, a faint female voice from inside: "Who is it, Merv?"

"Just some insurance geek."

She appeared beside him in the trailer doorway, wearing a tattered blue silk housecoat that, once upon a time, had come from some posh boutique. Even without makeup, and with her blonde hair tied starkly back in a dirty ribbon, I recognized her instantly. Elina.

At last, Elina.

Erle was grinning up at the couple, playing his role to perfection. But Elina was studying him with narrowed eyes.

"Who are you?" she demanded.

"Hiram Bixby," Erle repeated. "Service with a smile. That's our company motto." He tapped his briefcase. "As I was telling your husband, we're featuring—"

"Didn't I tell you to breeze?" Enright's glare was hot enough to melt glass.

"Yes, sir, but—"

"Who sent you here?" Elina's voice was laced with suspicion.

"Nobody, ma'am," said Gardner, maintaining his innocent tone. "I just thought that you might need—"

"You're gonna need a *doctor* if your ass isn't off this lot in the next ten seconds," snarled Enright. His fists were balled and the cords on his muscled neck were rigid.

Gardner backed away. "Sorry to have disturbed you folks. Maybe you'll be interested some other time." He turned and walked rapidly toward the street.

Behind him, the trailer door slammed shut with a bang.

Back in the alley, seated in my Duesenberg, the three of us had a conference. Gardner had been shaken by his encounter with Enright and kept wiping and rewiping his glasses.

"Right now," I said, "with things as they are, there's no way I'm going to be able to question Elina about Julian's death."

"That's assuming she knows something about it," put in Hammett.

"I assume nothing. But she's my only bet at the moment."

"And what about tying Enright to DuPlaine's murder?" asked Gardner.

"Nothing to be done there, either," I replied. "Not now, anyway. Elina may well suspect we're onto them."

"Her guard's up for sure," said Erle. He shook his head. "That Enright's a real hardcase . . . one mean bastard."

"Merv has to be out of the picture when you see Elina," Hammett said to me. "You'll have to get to her when she's alone."

"What good would that do? She wouldn't talk to me. We're the enemy, remember? She's on Enright's side."

"It's a tough situation," said Gardner. "What are you going to do?"

I turned to Hammett. "Can Buddy help?"

"What do you mean?"

"We need to keep an eye on Enright until I can work out an angle. He might decide to take off again—and we can't risk that.

147

Probably never find him. Could Buddy go on a stakeout?"

"For how long?"

"I don't know yet. Right now I've got to contact the Countess about finding her sister. After that, my obligation to her will end, and I'll be a free agent. Maybe then I can figure a way to reach Elina."

"So what do you want from me?" asked Hammett.

"There's a pool hall in that building," I said, indicating a red brick store complex across the street. "You can phone Buddy from there. Does he have transportation?"

"Besides the limo?"

"Yes."

"He has an old Buick coupe that he uses on his days off."

"Perfect," I said. "He can park the Buick across the street from the Crescent Moon and keep an eye on Enright's trailer—just to make sure Merv stays put."

"And when he leaves?"

"Buddy follows him and reports where he goes. If he makes a major move, then we'll know about it."

Hammett looked sour. "How do I get to the studio without a driver?"

"Use taxis," I said. "I'm depending on you, Dash. I need help. *Will* you phone Buddy?"

"Okay, I'll phone him—but this better not drag on for too long."

"Right now, it's one step at a time," I said. "And, Dash . . ."

"Yeah."

"I really appreciate the help. You're a pal."

He shrugged. "Guess we're all in this together. But to tell you the truth, I'm beginning to be sorry I ever introduced you to the Vampire Queen."

"Life is complex," I said. "We're just attempting to deal with some of its variegated complexities."

"Hah!" growled Hammett. "Spare me the philosophical crap."

I grinned. "Please . . . go call Buddy."

And he did.

FOURTEEN

A maid answered when I phoned the Countess in Hollywood. "Miss Carmilla" was out of town. I identified myself, saying I had some important information for the Countess, and where was she?

"Miss Carmilla is at the Hotel del Coronado."

"That's the one on Coronado Island, across from San Diego, right?"

"Yes, sir, that's where it is. Miss Carmilla is being specially honored there. It's a film festival, and they're showing her movies."

I thanked the maid and dialed the long-distance operator to connect the call. When the Hotel del Coronado answered, I asked to speak to Miss Blastok.

"I'm sorry, sir. That's not possible."

"Why?"

"Miss Blastok is not available right now. If you'd care to leave a message—"

"Forget it," I snapped, hanging up.

I didn't intend to sit around waiting for the Countess to call me. Time counted, and San Diego was not much more than a hundred miles south. I'd drive down there and find her.

I was alone in the house. When I'd arrived home after dropping off Hammett and Gardner I had found a note from Cissy, telling me that she and Margaret had gone to a concert at the Shrine Auditorium. I scrawled a quick note of my own, explaining my emergency trip and that I expected to return around noon the following day. I'd tell Cissy all about finding Enright when I got back. Maybe she'd have a bright idea on how I could get to Elina for the questions I needed to ask about Julian.

I felt guilty over the fact that Buddy was stuck watching Enright in Venice. It was an enormous imposition on him—and on Hammett. I wanted it over as soon as possible. It was, therefore, essential that I inform the Countess immediately regarding her sister.

Traffic was light and so I was able to keep the big Duesenberg rolling along at a solid speed. It's a great touring car, and I always enjoy its smooth power on the open road, but this particular drive to San Diego seemed to take forever.

My mind raced ahead of the car, filled with a dream tumble of unrelated images . . .

I thought about Julian's dead face at the morgue and about William Randolph Hearst standing in a shaft of sunlight at San Simeon and about Jack Snowden's lawn party and Bobbie Haining's con job at the house in Rialto and about Arnie's blackjack and Hedda Hopper's feathered hat and Art McQuillan's drifting smoke rings and the hard slash of rain at Julian's burial and the old geezer's bald head at the Grandview Apartments and Taki sleeping on my desk as I worked and Thelma Todd's garage in the fog and a punch in the stomach and a 12-gauge sawed-off and Charlie Chaplin's solemn face as he told me that vampires are real . . .

And, at last, I entered the San Diego city limits.

151

I found the dock with no trouble, and eased the Duesenberg over a long tongue of metal onto the Coronado ferry. The water in the bay was calm and dark, and the ferry cut across it like a knife slicing black oilcloth. The lights of Coronado glimmered ahead of us.

On the far side I got directions on how to reach the hotel, which was located on the beach at the other end of the island.

I'd seen many photographs of the Hotel del Coronado (a famous California landmark), but I wasn't prepared for the real thing. Rising five stories above the sand, the structure was eight-sided, with two rows of bay windows to each side, and was much vaster than the photos had indicated: an immense white wooden castle of cupolas, shingled towers, and hand-carved pillars, with a spreading red-canopied porte cochere at the gold-railed entrance.

Perched on a curving strand of beach fronting the Pacific, it had been built, if I remembered correctly, in the late 1880s, designed to serve king and commoner alike as one of the world's great seaside resort hotels. The Prince of Wales had once guested here, as had monarchs from Europe and the Orient. Al Capone was said to have planned several Chicago murders at the del Coronado, and Doug Fairbanks had been filmed climbing one of the towers as a publicity stunt.

A series of spotlights at ground level splashed rainbow colors across the tall wooden facade. At the hotel's front entrance a white cloth banner announced the film festival, with three lines, in blood red, at the bottom:

AND FEATURING, IN PERSON,
THE VAMPIRE QUEEN
CARMILLA BLASTOK!

I had a valet park my car and walked up a long stretch of immaculate threaded-gold carpet into a wide lobby jammed with chattering film fanatics. At least that was my assumption; who else would be crowding a hotel lobby at this late evening hour?

When I stepped up to the polished mahogany reception desk, a beaming clerk in an elegant black tuxedo told me how very fortunate I was. The place was booked solid, but . . .

"A cancellation has *just* come in for a lovely fifth-floor single overlooking the tennis courts," he said.

"Good," I nodded. "And on what floor is Miss Blastok?"

"Oh, the *first*, of course. With a lovely view of the ocean," he declared proudly. "It's our Royal Suite."

"Sounds lovely," I said, signing my name on the registration card.

He took down a large bronze key from a peg rack behind the desk. "I'll summon a boy for your luggage."

"I don't have any," I told him. "My trip was unexpected."

His eyebrows shot up and he nodded tightly. "Uh . . . yes sir, of course."

I'd been in such a hurry to reach the Countess that I had forgotten to pack an overnight bag. Well, that was the least of my problems. I could sleep in my underwear and get shaving gear from the concierge. The main thing was: I needed to find Carmilla.

She wasn't in the Royal Suite. When I found it, a hotel guard was standing in front of the door. He had a stout wooden "billy" belted to his hip, but I didn't see a gun. He was a squat, tough-looking character with a gold tooth lighting up his smile. I could tell he liked showing off the tooth because he smiled a lot.

"Help you, mister?" The gold tooth winked at me.

"My name is Raymond Chandler. I need to see Miss Blastok. She knows me, and she'll tell you it's okay to let me in."

"I'm sure she would if she was here," said the guard. "Trouble is, she isn't."

"Where is she?"

"In the ballroom," he said. "They're running *Bride of the Devil Bat* in there. Ever see it?"

"No," I said.

"Me, I saw it twice. Once in a movie theater when it first came out, and then later with my wife. Alma likes vampires. The blood and all, she likes it."

"How do I get to the ballroom?"

"There's dandy scene where the king devil bat makes her his bride. In some old house in the woods where everything's rotting. Dead rats on the floor. Real spooky. The vampire queen was dressed in this white wedding dress all smeared with blood, and she—"

"I really have to talk to Miss Blastok," I said, starting away. "I'm sure I can find the ballroom."

"Oh, you can't miss it," he said, giving me another flash of his gold tooth. "Straight down this hall, turn left, go through the lobby, and it'll be on your right. Real big room. The Countess will be answering questions from the audience. Got a few I wouldn't mind asking her myself. I'd show you the way, except I'm supposed to guard the door here and . . ."

He was still talking when I headed down the hall.

The ballroom was ink dark as I slipped inside. Full of Blastok lovers filling rows of wooden spectator chairs. A screen had been set up in front of the stage and the *Devil Bat* film was being projected on it.

I found an empty chair near the far wall and sat down. There was nothing I could do until the lights came on—and I had a mild curiosity about Carmilla's acting. Wanted to see for myself what made her so famous. So I began watching the screen action.

The film was in black and white and, according to McQuillan's file, had been directed by David DuPlaine. Actor Franchot Tone was the vampire hunter. I knew that because he was carrying a mallet and two sharpened wooden stakes. This scene was inside the devil bat's castle, with Tone leading a teenaged kid down a flight of dank steps. The boy was gripping a capped jar of clear liquid.

"We've got to hurry, Professor Hendrick," the boy was saying. "Once the sun is down, it'll be too late!"

A shot of the setting sun, almost to the horizon.

"Don't worry, Billy," said Tone, looking grim and strong-jawed. "We still have enough time left to put an end to this foul creature and his monstrous bride." He patted the boy's shoulder. "Just hang onto that jar of holy water. We might need it."

Now they were entering the castle's underground crypt. (What would a vampire picture be without a crypt?) A weak shaft of sunlight revealed two long pine coffins, side by side in the middle of the stone chamber. The production crew had laid in plenty of cobwebs.

They got the devil bat's coffin open first, with the camera going in for a close-up. Ugh! There was Bela Lugosi, eyes closed, his lips spattered with blood.

"Now!" said Billy. "*Hurry!*"

In went the sharpened stake. Bang! A blow from the mallet. Lugosi's eyes popped open in shock and he let out a frightful shriek. A stake in the chest isn't fun. Bang! Another strong blow from Tone's mallet and it was over. The chief devil bat had been dispatched.

Carmilla was next. As her coffin lid was pried off, the camera gave us the obligatory close-up. Beautiful, but deadly. Eyes closed. White pancake makeup. Long black hair (nice wig!). Delicate hands folded over her breasts.

Another shot of the sun. Just a thin yellow sliver at the horizon. Going . . . going . . . gone.

"Quick, Professor Hendrick! Strike now!"

Tone had the stake poised at Carmilla's chest and was about to drive it home when she surged up, screaming in fury, and grabbed him by the throat. He struggled against her clawed grip, but she was far too powerful. With a deep-throated grunt, she tossed him across the full length of the chamber.

Billy tried to run, but she pounced on him before he was able to reach the steps. The jar of holy water rolled out of his hand onto the stone floor.

Carmilla's eyes were blazing and a fanged smile made her look truly demonic. "Now, my sweet young innocent, you shall join the ranks of the Undead! I shall drink deeply of your crimson fluids!"

Her face lowered romantically into the camera and sharp, cat-like fangs filled the screen. I had to admit, she *was* impressive.

Then, with Billy powerless and quivering, Tone staggered to his feet, scooped up the jar of holy water, and ran at her, shouting: "Take this, you fiend from hell!" And, uncapping the jar, he tossed the contents into Carmilla's face.

It did the trick. With an agonized screech she fell away from Billy, clawing at her skin. Her nose and cheeks began to steam. She thrashed and twisted madly, screaming in pain.

In a well-executed special effect, Carmilla's flesh melted away to raw bone—leaving a motionless white skeleton on the stone floor.

Camera in on Tone's triumphant face as he hugged the boy. "That's the end of them both," he declared. "The reign of the devil bat and his loathsome bride is over. We're free, Billy! Free!"

Tears of joy ran down Billy's cheeks. The music swelled . . .

THE END

A thunder of applause as six overhead chandeliers bloomed into brightness, illuminating the huge ballroom. The crowd of at least two hundred clapped louder than ever as Carmilla stepped in front of an onstage microphone. She raised a hand for silence.

"Your appreciation of my art [no one laughed] is most gratifying," she told her fans. "I'm not sure that my work in *Bride of the Devil Bat* matched my performance in *Spawn of Dracula* [more applause], but I'm proud of what I did in this picture, and I'm *doubly* proud to be here with you tonight."

She went on for another ten minutes, telling the audience how much she valued their support and their love, and how she had worked hard, all through her career, to *earn* this love. Cornball blather, but they lapped it up.

By the time I reached her, behind the curtain of the small stage, she was in the middle of a thick circle of Blastok admirers, signing autographs and posing for photographers.

"Countess!" I shouted, waving my arms to get her attention. "Countess! It's *me!*"

Startled by my shouts, Carmilla swung her head in my direction. The crowd parted like the Red Sea as she beckoned me forward.

"Mr. Chandler! What are you doing here in Coronado?" She wore (naturally) a crimson gown, and her upper body flashed with jewelry. "And what happened to your jaw? It's all discolored."

"I found your sister," I said, ignoring her second question.

Her face bloomed like the chandeliers. "How wonderful!" Then, sudden concern: "Is she all right?"

"She's fine," I said.

I was being glared at by a ring of frustrated fans eager to obtain autographs. One of them, a sweating fat man in a checked suit, ducked under my left arm and thrust his program toward Carmilla. Smiling, she signed her name with a flourish.

"Is there somewhere we can talk?" I asked her.

"There's a bar downstairs," she said. "In the basement, actually. The Victorian Lounge. I'll meet you there just as soon as I

157

have satisfied the immediate demands of my public."

"Fine," I said.

As I stepped away, the Blastok fanatics closed in around the Countess like a starving wolf pack.

I was directed by a bellhop to a basement corridor leading to the lower barroom. It was a long corridor and I passed several historical displays—newspaper clippings, old photographs, mounted play programs, models of the area as it looked when the hotel had first been built in 1887, just eleven years after Custer took his fall at the Little Big Horn. Another time . . . another world.

I walked across an inlaid parquet floor into the Victorian Lounge. Potted plants. White wicker chairs. Stained glass windows and a fifty-foot bar with enough bottles displayed on the wall behind it to give the whole country a hangover.

I sat down in a booth upholstered in red leather and ordered a Scotch and soda.

A very tall, very thin man in milk-bottle glasses was staring at me from the next booth. I put up with this for a few minutes, then asked: "Do I know you?"

He instantly joined me, putting out a fleshless hand to shake. "You're Raymond Chandler, aren't you?"

I said yes. His eyes were enormous behind the thick lenses as he continued to stare at me.

"I saw your picture in the papers last year," he said. "When you and Mr. Hammett and Mr. Gardner were involved in shooting all those men at the beach."

"I didn't shoot anybody," I said. "I don't like guns."

"But there *was* shooting!" He looked angry, as if I had challenged his integrity. "You can't deny that!"

"Don't believe everything you read in the papers," I told him.

I picked up my Scotch and soda. "Now, if you'll excuse me, I'm waiting for someone."

I walked to the bar, taking a stool there. The thin guy shrugged, muttered something under his breath, and went back to his table. By the time the Countess arrived he'd ambled out, still muttering.

Carmilla took the stool next to mine, her eyes lit with anticipation. "So tell me everything."

And I did; I told her everything. About the attack in Culver City. About tracing the license plate to the Grandview and how this led to the Crescent Moon Trailer Court in Venice. And about Elina being with Merv.

"And she's all right?" the Countess asked.

"So far as I could tell," I said.

"Thank God!" Carmilla was trembling in the emotional aftermath of my news. "I was so desperately afraid that he might have . . ." She let the sentence die, but I knew what she meant.

"I guess she really *did* want her jewelry back," I said.

"I'll send you the remainder of your fee," she told me. "I'm not carrying much cash at present."

I nodded. "Now that you know where your sister is, what do you intend to do?"

"Well, I don't think she wants to talk to me," said the Countess. "She's made that perfectly clear."

"Then what *will* you do?"

"Nothing. You've accomplished my goal for me—to find Elina alive and well."

"But I thought you were worried about her being with Enright."

"I was. But there isn't anything I can do to separate them. And if she's all right after all this time, then I suppose the best thing is to just leave them alone."

"So it's over as far as you're concerned?"

"Yes. Over." She pressed a hand against my arm. "I thank you for finding her, Mr. Chandler. I knew my faith in you would be justified. You did a splendid job."

"It wasn't so splendid," I said. "If Merv Enright hadn't come after me—and if Hammett hadn't popped up when he did—then I doubt I'd have found your sister."

"That doesn't matter. The fact is, you *did* find her. You've restored my peace of mind."

"I'm happy to hear that," I said, thinking: I'd never sleep easy if I knew *my* sister was living with a creep like Enright. But the Countess was an odd bird, and I never try to figure odd birds.

Maybe the Countess was satisfied, but I wasn't. I still had to find a way of getting Elina alone so that I could question her about Julian Pascal.

So, for me, this definitely wasn't over.

FIFTEEN

Cissy met me at the door with a hug and a warm kiss when I returned from Coronado.

"Raymio! I was worried. I'm so glad you're home safe."

"You worry about me too much," I said, kissing her cheek. "I'm safe. Why wouldn't I be safe?"

"That dreadful man tried to kill you," she said. "It's no wonder I'm concerned."

"I found him."

"Who?"

"The dreadful man. Merv Enright. Buddy's watching his trailer in Venice right now."

I bent down to scratch Taki behind the ear. She bumped my leg, wrapping her tail around my knee.

"She's not used to having you gone," said Cissy. "She missed you."

"Sedentary writer becomes man of action." I smiled. "That's old Raymio."

"Is Carmilla Blastok's sister with this Enright person?"

I told her yes, and explained how frustrated I was at not being

161

able to talk to her. "How can I question Elina about Julian with her lethal boyfriend on the scene?"

"I can help," said Margaret, who stood in the hall doorway with a concerned frown on her face.

"How?" I asked. "How can you help?"

"She'll probably talk to another woman," declared Margaret. "Especially after she knows who I am—that I was so close to Julian. I'll phone and say I want to meet her alone, outside the trailer park, to discuss Julian. She'll go out of curiosity if nothing else. Then I'll try to find out if she knows anything about his suicide."

"Murder," corrected Cissy tartly. "It was murder."

Margaret's eyes were intense on mine. "Do you really think Elina Knibbs might be involved in what happened to Julian?"

"No, no." I shook my head. "I don't think that at all. But maybe . . . in some way . . . *Enright* was connected with Julian's death. I don't pretend to know how."

"But even if this is true," said Cissy, "why would Elina admit it? She'd never implicate the man she's romantically involved with."

"At the moment, we don't know *what* she'll say." I turned to Margaret. "I like your idea . . . about meeting with Elina. But first I want to talk to Buddy and find out what the present situation is. So hold off your phone call until I give you the go-ahead."

"Whatever you think is best," said Margaret. Her eyes darkened. "Is Buddy all right? Is someone helping him watch the trailer? He can't be there twenty-four hours a day."

"Erle promised to have Tomas, his houseboy, help out," I said. "I'll tell Buddy you asked about him."

"Don't you dare!" Margaret smiled. "He'll think I'm being forward."

"Nerts to that," I said. "He'll be delighted. Buddy thinks

you're something special." I gave her a hug. "And you are. *Very* special."

Back in Venice I parked in the same alley, took a brown paper bag from the seat beside me, and walked to the Crescent Moon. A slight spring breeze rustled the silvered green leaves of the eucalyptus trees, and the intense clear blue of the subtropical sky was a benison. The faint, briny smell of the Pacific reached me and I inhaled it like perfume; I've always loved being near the ocean . . . of being at the edge of something vast and mysterious.

Buddy was parked across the street in a dusty gray Buick coupé, rust-pitted, with a large dent in the right front fender. From his vantage point, he had a clear view of Enright's trailer in the lot beyond the fence.

"How's it going?" I asked, opening the passenger door and slipping into the front seat next to him. He looked upset.

"I've been sitting here trying to figure out what to do," he told me. "I needed to talk to you, but I didn't want to leave Merv Enright alone while I took time to phone."

"What's wrong?"

"About two hours ago Enright and the woman left," Buddy related. "I followed them to the Safeway; it's about a mile south on Venice Boulevard. I parked on the far side of the lot and waited for them. They came out with two bags of groceries, but they didn't go back to their trailer."

"Where *did* they go?"

"They stopped off at an Owl for some ice cream at the soda fountain. Malted milks. Stayed in there for about forty minutes. Then they came home."

"So why call me about any of this?"

"Because of what happened while they were gone," said Buddy. "Somebody had been here."

"Been where?"

"In their trailer," said Buddy. "I heard Enright yelling and cursing shortly after they got back, so I sneaked through the gap in the fence and crawled around behind his truck. The back window of the trailer was open and I could see inside. A mess. Looked like a hurricane had hit the place. Somebody had gone through everything."

"And that's what all his yelling was about?"

"Yes. He was plenty upset. But whoever did it *didn't* get what they came for."

"How do you know that?"

"Because I watched Enright take apart a section of the air vent in the ceiling and remove a small package. Wrapped in white butcher paper, tied with string. He was really happy it was still there."

"Did he open the package?"

"No. Just slipped it inside the vent, then put the grate back."

"Did he talk to Elina about the contents?"

"No, not a word. She just stood there, looking. I decided it was too risky for me, being out there in the lot in broad daylight, so I sneaked back here to the car. And then you showed up."

I rubbed a hand along my chin. "I'd love to know what's in that package."

"Whatever it is, someone sure *wanted* it," said Buddy.

"This doesn't change anything," I said. "We still have to keep watching Enright. Can't chance his leaving. That package just adds one more element to the equation."

"So I stay here?"

"Yeah. Until Tomas, comes to spell you."

"He's doing a good job," said Buddy. "I don't know how I could handle this all alone."

"You seem to be holding up okay." I suddenly remembered the brown paper bag. "Margaret thought you might be hungry, so she packed you a lunch."

He smiled so broadly I thought his cheeks would split. "I am. Thank her for me, please . . ."—his eyes were shining—"until *I* can thank her, in person."

"I'll do that," I said. "Do you need anything? Maybe a rest room?"

"No, thanks. I used the one in the Flying-A station next to the drugstore when they were getting their malts."

I told Buddy how much I appreciated what he was doing, and that I'd be checking with him later. I wanted to confer with Margaret and plan out exactly what she'd say to Elina on the phone.

That didn't happen.

When I got back to the Duesenberg, Enright's two muscle boys were waiting for me. Arnie had the blackjack in his hand.

And this time he used it.

A swirling haze, pierced by a burning sun in the middle of the sky. The haze thinned as I got the sun in partial focus. Shimmering there in the sky in a double image. No, not in the sky. In the ceiling. And it wasn't a sun, it was a hanging glass bowl supported by rusted link chains with two glowing bulbs inside.

I was lying on my back in a narrow iron bed, on a thin mattress filled with lumps of coal. At least it felt that way. Wearing a pair of faded blue flannel pajamas a size too small, my ankles and wrists poking out at each end.

I sat up. Not easy. The room tipped and swayed like a ship in heavy seas and I had to grip the edge of the bed for balance. Sat there blinking. My head hurt. Felt it. Sore. Very sensitive. Hair matted. Maybe with blood? My face itched. Ran a hand over my cheek. Stubble. I'd been here for several hours.

Where was here?

A room. Gray walls, gray ceiling, gray floor. Wooden chair in the center. Window on the far wall. Closet with the door closed.

Washstand with a sink in one corner. Bottle on it. Johnnie Walker. Hammett's favorite.

I needed a drink.

Gripping the edge of the bed, I stood up. *Tried* to stand up. Whoa! The room started dancing under me. Around and around she goes, and where she stops, nobody knows.

My legs were full of champagne bubbles. Knees watery. And my bare feet were unhappy. This guy wants to stand on us! He's got a nerve, he has. My legs agreed. Yeah, why should *we* have to support him? I told them to shut up and do their job.

I was standing. Weaving like a drunk at a country picnic, I made it to the chair. Hooray for me! Old rubber legs Chandler is on the move. I stood there, holding onto the chairback, while the room kept doing its number.

The bottle of Johnnie Walker winked at me. C'mon over, pal, and have a swig. Do you good. Put some lead in your pencil. Said the duchess to the bishop.

The trip from chair to washstand was tough going but I finally got there. One hand braced on the washstand, other hand on the bottle. Thank God it was uncapped. I curled my fingers around the neck of the bottle and tipped it upward, toward my open mouth. Spilled a lot before getting the angle right. Ah, at last! Swallowed. Swayed. Began coughing. Dropped the bottle. It rolled, spitting whiskey.

The wooden floor reached up and smacked me in the face.

Doped. Whiskey was doped. Which was why I couldn't get things in focus. Someone had poured doped booze into me. Bastards! They should have known I needed to finish my story for Joe Shaw. No time to be lying face down on some wooden floor in some room in some building somewhere. Had to work on my story. Lot of pages to do. Taki, get off my papers! Scoot! Can't write with you sprawled across my papers.

Water. Needed cold water. To help clear my head. Never

166

should have swallowed that whiskey. Made things worse.

Up again. Blood on my lip. Tastes salty. On my knees. I made a lunge for the sink. Almost fell. Slow down, Chandler. You'll end up flat on your ass if you don't take it easy. Slow and easy, attaboy! Using the edge of the washstand, I pulled myself to a standing position. Faced the sink. Chipped enamel. Rusted faucets. Did they work? Turned a handle. A groan from the pipes . . . then water. *Cold* water!

I lowered my head under the stream from the faucet, letting the water splash over my face and hair, running down my neck and shoulders to soak my pajama top. Turned it off. Felt better. Stronger. Still woozy, though. Dope isn't that easy to shake. They'd done a job on me, all right. At least I could get things in focus. And the room had settled down; guess it got tired of doing the tango. Or maybe the storm at sea was over.

Then I thought about the window. A way out. An exit point. I started for it, swayed, steadied myself, got going again—and there I was. At the window.

Lower floor. View of a yard . . . trees . . . two-door wooden garage in back. The window was locked, but that didn't matter. With a supreme effort I could probably use the chair to smash out the glass pane. But that wouldn't help. A closer inspection revealed an iron grating on the outside that made an exit impossible.

"Can't get out that way, Raymio," a calm voice said behind me. Nobody ever called me Raymio but Cissy. Her special name. It had to be Cissy!

But it wasn't. It was Erle Gardner. Had his bow with him, the arrows in a leather case at his waist. He wore a woodsman's outfit, with high boots and a wide-brimmed hat. There was a magenta feather in the hat.

"Who you been hunting, Erle?" I asked him.

"Dreadful people," he said. "World's full of 'em."

"I'm mighty glad to see you, partner," I said. "I was getting depressed. Couldn't imagine how I'd ever get out of here."

"There's a way out," nodded Erle.

"Where am I, anyhow? What *is* this place?"

"*Hell*, Raymio, that's what it is. You're in the dreadful place."

"But you know a way out?"

He smiled, looking avuncular. "There's a way out of everything."

"I mean, out of *this* place."

"What's the hurry?" He raised his bow. "Don't you want me to kill some of the dreadful people who brought you here?"

"No—I just want to get out. I don't want anybody killed."

"Okay, then, Raymio," he said. "Just follow me."

Gardner moved to the closet door, opened it, and walked inside, shutting the door behind him. Now, why had he done that?

I had a little trouble getting over there. Opened the door. My clothes were inside, tossed on the floor with my shoes. Otherwise, the closet was empty.

Erle was gone.

Rotten thing for a pal to do, leaving me behind like this. I was angry. Damn the man!

"You can't always trust your friends," said another voice. Female. I turned to confront Carmilla.

The Countess was in black. In her long black cape. She even wore black lip rouge, the way actors did in silent films. Her green eyes were black, too, and her fingernails. Black. Deep midnight black.

"How did you find me?" I asked her.

"The ethers," she said. "I simply tuned in to your ethers and they led me here, to you. Is that so difficult to understand?"

"No, no it isn't, not at all. Makes sense." I stared into her black eyes. They seemed to lack pupils. Just a fathomless, unbroken field of darkness. "What are you doing here, Carmilla? Why have you come?"

"To comfort you." Her lips curved in a thin, mirthless smile. "To ease your mental pain."

"That's very kind of you," I said.

"Your pajamas are wet," she told me. "They don't fit. You look ridiculous."

"I know. They aren't mine. My clothes are in the closet."

"Too bad your Duesenberg isn't in there," she said. "You could drive away in it."

"Closet's too small," I declared. "My Duesenberg is big. Too big for a Chinese cemetery. Back wheels run over the graves."

"Vampires aren't afraid of graves," she told me. "We just claw our way out once the sun is down. Right out, through the dirt and the worms and the maggots."

"I've never believed in them," I said. "In vampires, I mean."

"We don't care whether people believe in us or not. We exist." She stepped closer to me. Very close. I could feel her hot breath on my skin.

"You have blood on your lip," she said, very softly. Her eyes held tiny pinpoints of fire in their depths, a shimmering black fire.

"I cut myself . . . when I hit the floor."

"Let me have it," said Camilla, leaning forward. Her tongue slipped out, snakelike, between her blackened teeth, and she licked the blood away. "There." A deep sigh. "Isn't that better?"

I was staring at her, unable to speak.

"I shall leave you now," she said. "Before the sun rises."

Through the window, the edge of the sky was faintly tinged with pink.

"Can't I go with you?" I asked.

"No, that's impossible. Farewell, Mr. Chandler."

And to my horror and amazement her body began folding in on itself, compressing, altering, until . . .

A great leathery black bat, with red-coal eyes, yawned its fanged mouth wide in a high-pitched scream, pivoted in the air, and darted for the window, passing through the glass and out.

Into the still-dark morning.

SIXTEEN

I *had* to get out.

Adrenaline surged in my veins. I was frantic to escape. Had to get out. Had to! *Had to!*

I picked up the wooden chair and attacked the window, shattering the glass and cross frame, battering at the rusted iron grating.

A rattling sound of keys, of thrown bolts. The door swung open. Arnie stood braced in the doorway, the leather blackjack in his hand. "What do you think you're doin', wise guy?"

"Damn you!" I snarled. "You put me here!"

"I just followed orders. Enright calls the shots. He was real unhappy about the way you trashed his place, so he told me and Al to grab you."

"I had nothing to do with his trailer," I said, breathing fast. "That was someone else."

"Uh-huh," nodded Arnie. "Merv, he figures different."

"Where is he?"

"Be here soon enough. Had some things to take care of."

"Is he going to kill me?"

"Maybe. Maybe not." Arnie grinned. "Won't know 'til he

gets here. Al went to fetch him." He hefted the blackjack. "Meantime, boyo, I'm gonna have to put you back to sleep."

He moved toward me, still grinning. Arnie enjoyed using a sap and he rated me an easy target. He didn't expect to have any trouble with a doped-up sedentary writer.

I surprised him.

I hit him with the chair. Smashed him to the floor. When he got to one knee, I brought the chair down again. Hard. He didn't move after that.

I swayed toward the closet, suddenly weak and dizzy. The room began to tilt and swing.

I had to put one hand against the wall to keep from falling. Closed my eyes. Stood there for a minute or two, breathing deeply, trying to regain strength and balance. Better. Stronger now. Vital that I get out fast. No telling when Al and Merv Enright would arrive.

Cold morning air from the window hit me as I stripped off the sweat-laden pajamas. Shivering, I pulled on my shirt and trousers, a real struggle in my weakened condition. Sat down on the bed to put on my shoes. Didn't bother with socks.

Arnie still hadn't moved. He was sprawled on his back. I could see his chest lifting slightly with each breath. Just knocked out. Maybe with a concussion—but he wasn't dead. Good. I'm no killer.

Hallway beyond the room. Through that into a rancid grease-smelling kitchen, then out the broken screen door to the backyard. Staggering most of the way, bumping walls, fighting the woozy feeling in my head, but making solid progress.

I was praying my Duesenberg was in that garage. Too valuable for them to abandon, and too conspicuous to leave on the street. I looked back at the house: big gingerbread Victorian job, with full corner bay windows, spindle turrets, and a wide wooden porch running halfway around it. The room I'd been locked inside was part of a newer annex built onto the main structure; from the yard, through the shattered window and its iron grating, I could see the ceiling light globe, still glowing.

The garage doors were closed, but not locked. I dragged them open, gasping and shaky. Peered inside. And there she was, snug and safe in the dim early morning light. Sweetest sight in creation.

My Duesenberg.

I climbed behind the wheel, fired the engine, released the brake, and backed out. Bumped over some yard rocks, reached the street, and gunned away. No sign of Enright. A clean escape.

The area was familiar. Bunker Hill, the legendary turn-of-the-century residential area just north of City Hall. To my right, the funicular cable railway clattered loudly up the steeply angled clay bluff from Hill Street, its seats empty in the dawn stillness of the wakening city.

My first thought was McQuillan. See him. Tell him about my kidnapping, that I'd been doped and slated for possible murder. But I had no proof that Merv Enright was behind it, just the word of a sap-happy mug whose testimony wouldn't be worth a wooden dime.

Then I thought about Buddy. Enright obviously knew Buddy was watching him by the time I arrived. Probably saw him head back to the Buick after his side trip to the trailer. Called in Arnie and Al and had them grab me. But what had he done to Buddy? Could he be dead by now? An iced chill ran down my spine.

I headed for a pay phone.

Hammett didn't know anything.

"Did Buddy call in?" I asked him.

"Nope. Haven't heard from him. We'd better get out there. Can you pick me up?"

"On the way," I said.

From Hammett's place in the Palisades it took us about fifteen minutes to get to the Crescent Moon.

The Buick was still parked in the same spot under the trees— but Buddy wasn't in it.

"That son of a bitch has killed him!" I said, banging a fist against the side of the car.

"No sense in jumping to conclusions," warned Hammett. "We need to check things out. Let's go for the trailer."

I'm sure that Dash was equally upset, but he didn't show it. Emotionally, he always holds himself on a tight rein; maybe this strict control was acquired in his years with Pinkerton. One of Hammett's major problems in his broken marriage to Jose was his inability to express deep feelings. He hated saying the words "I love you." And that's death in a relationship; a woman has to be told she counts, that she's wanted and loved. Dash has always had trouble talking about things like that. He can't tolerate any form of sentimentality. It works for him in his writing—that cold, spare style of expression—but not nearly so well in his personal life.

We slipped through the gap in the wooden slat fence and walked directly up to Enright's trailer. We knew that he wasn't inside. By now, he'd no doubt arrived at the house on Bunker Hill to find Arnie with a king-sized headache, and no Chandler.

The door gaped open and we stepped in, expecting to find the trailer empty. It wasn't. A body lay face down on the cracked linoleum floor.

Buddy.

Hammett knelt to check his pulse. "Alive," he said. "Give me a hand with him."

We lifted Buddy onto a narrow bed built into the back wall. The trailer had been stripped and the stained blue-tick mattress was bare, but it was a lot better than the floor.

Inside, I was smiling like a kid at Christmas. If Enright *had* killed Buddy, I would have borne the full responsibility for his death, since this stakeout idea had been mine. But thank God I was off the hook; he was okay.

"He's beginning to come out of it," said Hammett, who was chafing Buddy's wrists to restore circulation. "Got a nasty cut on his forehead, but at least it's stopped bleeding."

Buddy fluttered his eyes open, bringing Hammett into focus. "Hey . . . Chief . . . am I glad to see you!"

"Likewise," said Dash, grinning at him.

Then Buddy saw me. "Hi, Ray!"

"Hi, pal," I said. "How're you feeling?"

He tried to sit up, but fell back against the mattress. "Not good. What happened?"

"Enright spotted us," I told him. "When I left you yesterday, his two apes grabbed me. They sapped me, forced me to drink doped whiskey, and then they locked me in a house on Bunker Hill. Our boy Merv was on the way there when I managed to bust out."

"Ray played hero," said Hammett. "Conked ole Arnie with a chair."

"Très bien," murmured Buddy.

"I got lucky," I said. "I just wanted to get the hell out any way I could."

Hammett put a hand on Buddy's shoulder. "What about you? How did you end up here?"

"I don't know," said Buddy. "I remember sitting in the Buick. I heard a noise behind me. I turned around, and—wham! Somebody cracked me over the head. It must have been Merv Enright. Then I guess he dragged me here."

"Probably wanted to question you," I said. "But when you didn't wake up, he had to leave."

"Do you figure Elina is still with him?" Dash asked me.

"Sure. She goes where *he* goes."

Buddy was staring intently toward the ceiling.

"What are you looking at?" asked Hammett.

"Air vent," said Buddy. "That's where he kept the package hidden. It could still be up there."

"Not a chance," said Hammett. "Obviously it's valuable if somebody wanted it badly enough to ransack this trailer for it. Enright would never leave it behind."

I checked to make certain, with Buddy directing my efforts. Dash was right; the space inside the vent was empty.

Hammett had been poking through a wastebasket near the door when I said, "Looks like he took everything with him."

"Not everything," said Dash, holding up a crumpled bit of paper.

"What's that?" I asked.

"A pawn ticket," he said.

Ronald's Pawn Emporium—which was what the owner insisted on calling it—was in Santa Monica, a few blocks from the ocean off Fifth Street. It nestled between a family barbershop, with an autographed poster of Babe Ruth in the window ("Use Wildroot Cream Oil to Keep Every Hair in Place!"), and Bernie's Second-Day Bakery, where you could get a loaf of yesterday's bread for eight cents and two packages of Hostess cupcakes for a nickel. Depression prices, if you didn't mind stale food.

Hammett was with me. After regaining his strength, Buddy had driven his Buick back to Hammett's house in the Palisades.

The interior of the pawnshop was typical—a dust-cloaked jumble of trumpets, guitars, radios, cameras, jewelry, pocket watches, slide trombones, typewriters, fur coats, violins, hunting rifles, bicycles, grandfather clocks, and kitchenware. A fat brass tuba was propped next to the cash register, just in front of a dusty shelf of derbies and top hats.

Ronald himself stood behind the counter, a stumpy little man, round as a pork barrel. A white nose hair you could string a harp with grew out of his left nostril and he had a mole on his neck big enough to hang your hat on. In the dimness of his pawnshop he smelled dank and musty, as if the sun hadn't touched him for weeks. His eyes watered as he talked to us and he sniffled a lot.

"Got me a terrible cold," he complained. "Can't seem to shake it. I caught it from my dog. Can you catch cold from a dog?"

"I don't think so," I said.

Hammett handed him the smoothed-out ticket. "A friend of mine, Mervin Enright, gave this to me," he declared. "Merv says he pawned some stuff with you."

"Well . . . lemme see . . ." Ronald licked his forefinger and checked a grease-stained receipt book on the counter.

"Enright . . . Enright . . . Yup, here he is. Brought in some jewelry. Nothing much. Five rings and a bracelet. A broach, a pearl necklace . . . I gave him a real fair price."

"Was one of the pieces a rose-gold lady's watch?" I asked.

"Yup. That was kinda nice. Best piece in the bunch."

I remembered that Carmilla had mentioned the watch when she told me what she'd sent to Enright. Apparently he'd taken everything directly here.

"Where's the jewelry now?" Hammett wanted to know.

"Downtown," said Ronald. "Enright was supposed to pay me interest if he wanted it back. When I didn't get my first payment, I sent the stuff downtown—to another store I work with. Maybe it's still there."

"Uh-huh," said Hammett.

"Did he tell you where he *got* the jewelry?" I asked.

"Naw. Probably belonged to his wife, maybe his mother or grandmother. It's like the first time he came in: I didn't ask, he didn't tell me."

Hammett's eyes flashed. "The *first* time? You mean he was in here earlier with something else?"

"Yup . . . now that I remember him. Came in about three years back with some silver goods. Half-dozen bowls, a nice dinner set. Quality stuff. He never sent me the interest payments on those either, so I sold all of 'em." He grinned. "Made me a real nice profit."

My hunch was vindicated. The silver stolen from the home of David DuPlaine had ended up here in Santa Monica. Pawned by the man who shot him to death.

Merv Enright.

SEVENTEEN

The Countess was in her swimming pool, taking an afternoon dip, when I walked up to her.

According to the magazine and newspaper articles I'd read, when *Curse of the Vampire* had become such a big box office success, David DuPlaine had shown his appreciation for his leading lady's work by arranging for studio set designers to transform Carmilla's backyard into a tropical paradise.

The pool, irregularly shaped and paved in smooth river rock, was designed to look as if it were an accidentally formed tropical rain pond nestled on some isle in Polynesia. A tall granite waterfall gently sprayed mist in the air, providing much-needed humidity for fragrant plumeria and stephanotis bushes. The brilliant flame-colored flowers of a Royal Poinciana and the intense lavender-blue of a flowering jacaranda formed a bright contrast to the deep, symmetrical green of a giant monkeypod tree. Around the perimeter, property lines were marked by coconut palms interspersed with shrubs of red hibiscus and white pikake. If you couldn't take a cruise to Hawaii, this certainly was the next best thing.

Out of her dark clothing and without her carefully applied

makeup, the Countess had shed her vampire menace. In a plain navy blue swimming suit, the kind used by athletic teams, Carmilla Blastok was revealed as a rather unattractive middle-aged woman with flabby arms and varicose veins. The bright California sun was anything but kind to her sags, wrinkles, and emerging gray hair roots.

After backstroking to the edge of the pool, she stood up at the shallow end, looking at me with surprised eyes. "Mr. Chandler! I certainly didn't expect to see you here."

"Consider this an impromptu visit," I said, taking a large towel from a white bent-cane plantation chair and handing it to her as she climbed out of the water.

"Thank you," she said, drying herself. She put on a white terry cloth robe and we sat down at an enameled table under a yellow-striped umbrella. I declined her offer of iced limeade as she poured herself a glass from a pitcher on the table.

"You must have come through the back gate. I thought I'd locked it."

"You did. I *unlocked* it. Little trick Dash Hammett taught me."

"How clever," she said in a mocking tone. "And what did you do about Bruno? As you know, he *does* tend to use his teeth on intruders who enter my property."

"I brought along some raw hamburger. Bruno decided to use his teeth on that."

Her eyes narrowed. "You realize that you *are* an intruder?"

"I plead guilty to the charge." I smiled at her. "However, under the circumstances, I thought I'd just pop in unannounced."

"*What* circumstances? If you're here for money, I have already mailed you the remainder of your fee."

"I'm not here about money."

"Then why *are* you here, Mr. Chandler?"

I leaned back in the chair, crossing my legs. "I had a kind of waking nightmare about you. You might call it a vision. Quite revealing, actually."

She was toweling her damp hair. "Do tell me about it."

"You were all in black. Even your eyes were black. You became excited when you saw some blood on my lip and proceeded to lick it off. Then you turned into a large bat and flapped away."

"Heavens!" she said. "That vampire film of mine in Coronado must have had a much greater influence on you than I'd imagined."

"Maybe it was a warning. From my subconscious. A warning not to trust you, that you're not exactly what you appear to be."

She laughed. "You mean, perhaps I really *am* a vampire?"

"No, my vision was symbolic. It meant that you are pretending to be something you aren't."

"How very cryptic," she said. "There must be a point to all this. Surely you didn't invade my property to tell me about some . . . vision you had."

I nodded. "You're right, I didn't. But it's related. Because of you, I was almost murdered."

She frowned. "Mr. Chandler, you're talking melodramatic nonsense. Whatever happened to you had nothing to do with me."

"Wrong!" I gave her a hard look. "It had *everything* to do with you." I hesitated, holding in my anger. "You set me up, lady. You lied about why you wanted me to locate your sister."

She started to protest, but I kept on: "You knew all along that Elina was living with Enright, but you didn't know *where*. So you used me to find out."

"But why would I—"

"So you could break into Enright's place when he wasn't there and search for something he had that you wanted." By now I was glaring at her. "Merv was very upset about the break-in. He figured you sent *me* to ransack his trailer—which nearly cost me my life."

She stood up. "I don't know whether or not you drink in the afternoon, Mr. Chandler, but right now I need something stronger than limeade."

I followed her through a wide French door to a bar in the game room. She asked me what I'd have and I shook my head. I wasn't there to socialize over cocktails. Carmilla fixed herself a Scotch on the rocks and we sat down again. I had a lot to find out about.

"I'm truly sorry for what happened to you," she said. "I didn't expect Enright to turn violent. I won't deny that you are correct in blaming me."

"Then, you admit it . . . you *did* search that trailer?"

She nodded.

"Looking for what?"

"I can't tell you that."

"Then maybe you'd like to tell the police."

She put her glass down hard on the coffee table, splashing Scotch. "Why are you threatening me? I paid you a handsome sum for doing what I asked of you. You accepted my money. Why can't you let it go at that?"

"Did you ever read *The Maltese Falcon?*"

"No. Why?"

"There's a detective named Spade in it. He doesn't like being played for a sap. Neither do I."

"I told you everything you needed to know in order to find my sister. There are . . . factors . . . that do not concern you."

I smiled tightly. "Such as David DuPlaine's murder?"

The color drained from her face. She literally reeled back, as if I'd struck her. "David was . . . shot by a burglar."

"Sure," I said. "A burglar named Merv Enright."

She fought to regain composure. "You are very wrong about that, Mr. Chandler. I can assure you that Enright had nothing to do with David's death."

"I talked to a friend of Merv's, a girl named Bobbie Haining. She said that Enright considered DuPlaine a phony, that they'd had an argument once at a dinner party."

"Even if that's true, it means nothing," Carmilla declared. "What proof do you have that Enright had anything to do with David's death?"

"The silver," I said.

She stared at me.

"Several bowls and a dinner set—taken by the killer on the night DuPlaine died. Enright pawned them in Santa Monica. I checked with the shop owner. He dealt directly with Enright. Elina's boyfriend shot DuPlaine. There's no doubt of it."

The Countess sighed, lowering her eyes. "Poor David! He didn't deserve to die like that." She lifted her gaze to me. "He was an incredible talent, a man of true genius."

"Funny how life goes," I said. "Here you were feeding me a lot of crap about being afraid that Enright might kill your sister, and the one he *really* killed was your lover."

She whirled, pointing a long-nailed finger at me. Her voice was shrill: "That is a foul lie! David and I were never—"

"Your ex-husband filled me in on the details," I said. "Even showed me a photograph he took of you and DuPlaine in bed together. Real cozy."

"Damn you, Chandler!" Her tone was colder than the ice in her glass.

"Apparently David DuPlaine did a lot more for you than direct your pictures."

She walked stiffly to the patio door, throwing it open. "I want you to leave my house. Now!"

"We aren't finished yet," I told her. "What were you looking for in Enright's trailer?"

"That's not your concern."

"It *becomes* my concern when I nearly get killed over it. What's in the package, Carmilla? And why did you go after it? Must be pretty important. If Enright had caught you going through his trailer—"

"Get out or I'll put the dog on you!" Her green eyes were burning. "He'll attack at my command."

"Not today, he won't," I said, giving her a grin. "Bruno's sleeping off the hamburger. I added a little something extra to the meat."

"You have no legal right to be here," she said hotly. "You're trespassing. I *insist* that you leave immediately."

I walked to the open patio door.

"Okay, I'll leave . . . for now. But our business isn't finished. And it won't be until I've had some questions answered."

I moved across the tiled patio toward the gate, pausing to look back at her.

The bluster was gone. Carmilla Blastok was a very frightened woman.

When Cissy heard the full story of my adventures on Bunker Hill she was ready to call President Roosevelt and have him send the National Guard after Enright. I calmed her down, saying I was perfectly okay and that all the rough stuff was over.

"How can you make a statement like that?" Cissy demanded. "He's out there somewhere in this city right now, and he'll go after you again. He probably thinks you've found out that he shot David DuPlaine."

"Which I have."

"Yes, yes, that's the whole *point!* He'll try to murder you to keep you from testifying against him."

"The silver has all been sold, so there's no tangible evidence—just the word of an old pawnbroker."

"But Enright won't care about tangible evidence," she said. "He'll come after you again! I'm very worried about you."

"You always worry about me. You worry about me getting fat. Or not getting enough exercise. Or not eating the right food. Or not getting enough sleep. Or working too hard!"

"But this is different," she protested. "All I wanted you to do was find out the truth about Julian's death. God knows I didn't want you to get hurt."

"His death is part of it. I don't know how Julian's death fits in, but I'm certain it's connected. When you write detective stories, you learn to connect things."

"You appear so confident, but I fail to see any basis for your confidence. It seems to me you're being just plain foolhardy."

I gave her a hug. "I've got to see Dash and Erle. Promise me you'll relax and *try* not to worry. Okay?"

"Nonsense. Of *course* I'll worry."

That's my Cissy. No false promises for her. If there's worrying to be done, she's right in there doing it, God love her!

"So . . . where do we go from here?" asked Gardner.

We were seated in the rumpus room in the basement of Hammett's house in Pacific Palisades. Dash had whomped up three tall strawberry sodas made with big scoops of C.C. Brown's vanilla and they were delicious. Double-dip ice cream sodas on a almost-summery spring evening. Perfect.

I answered Erle's question with one of my own: "How do you guys feel about the Countess?"

"She's nuts," said Hammett flatly. "She's also dangerous."

"How so?" I asked.

"You want something, you don't break into somebody's trailer to get it," he said, poking at his soda with a straw. "And

185

you don't set up writers to get sapped and kidnapped."

"She didn't expect Enright to try anything violent with me," I pointed out.

"The guy's a murderer," said Hammett. "Murderers tend to be violent."

"Carmilla doesn't believe that Merv shot DuPlaine. When I mentioned the stolen silver, it was a big shock to her."

"I don't think we can be sure of what she believes or doesn't believe," declared Hammett. "She's an actress, so who's to know when she's giving a performance? You're too gullible, Chandler."

"And you're too cynical," I countered.

Hammett stared at me. "My God, Ray, she lied to you, played you like a puppet on a string, and nearly got you croaked! Isn't that enough to convince you she's dangerous?"

"Maybe it should be," I admitted. "But in a way I feel sorry for her. She's lost DuPlaine, her sister, *and* her career. That's a lot to lose."

"Chandler the Romantic," grinned Hammett. "You should be riding a white horse instead of a Duesenberg."

"I repeat my question, gentlemen," said Erle. "Where do we go from here?"

"We stake out Carmilla's house," I said. "We follow her. She may lead us to Enright and Elina."

"How do you figure that?" asked Gardner. "She needed *you* to find them before. How could she do it on her own?"

"It's very possible that he will find *her*," I said. "He's been flushed out, into the open. He may be afraid it will happen again. He's got something she wants very badly—and he just might contact her."

"That's a long shot," said Hammett. "I don't like the idea of another stakeout. The last one cost Buddy a bashed skull. And it *could* have been worse."

"I'll watch her place," said Gardner. "Tomas can spell me. I'm writing a stakeout scene in my latest Ed Jenkins, so this will give me some practical experience. But if nothing happens in the next couple of days . . ."

"Thanks, Erle, I appreciate that," I told him. "I think something *will* happen."

"Another gut hunch?" asked Hammett.

"Could be," I said.

"Okay, then . . ." Dash said, setting his empty soda glass on the counter. "You guys play detective. Me, I'll stick with my chores at Global. I've been getting a lot of pressure on the vampire script; they want it finished as soon as possible."

"If something breaks, I may need you," I told him.

"Swell," he said. "You always know where to find me." He shot me a crooked half-smile. "Which is more than you can say for Merv Enright."

I finished my soda and we left it at that.

EIGHTEEN

I lay in our darkened bedroom, with Cissy sleeping deeply beside me, the warm weight of her body a solid comfort in the night. The clock on the bedtable said it was midnight, but it might as well have been high noon for all the sleep I was getting. My muscles were taut; I couldn't relax.

I could feel the pulse of my heart beating in conjunction with the ticking clock. I shifted position, rolling over on my right side, burrowing deeper into the pillow. I was experiencing a sense of apprehension, of forces beyond my control gathering toward a climax, pulling me into a whirlpool of danger.

The minutes ticked away until, finally, I drifted off . . . into nightmare.

I was with the Countess at the Hotel del Coronado once again, watching another of her gore-spattered vampire epics. But this time the two of us were alone in the vast ballroom; the chairs around us were empty. In the reflected light from the screen, Carmilla's face was stark and angular, the glow of her intense green eyes like points of emerald fire in the darkness.

She leaned close to me, her voice a sinister whisper in my ear:

"He's waiting for you, Mr. Chandler. He wants you to join him."

"Who? *Who's* waiting for me?"

"Come." She stood up, taking my hand. Her fingers were cold.

The Countess led me to the front of the room. I stood there, at the foot of the stage, looking up at the flickered images. It was storming onscreen; thunder sent a lion's rumble through the night sky. Lightning speared and sizzled, illuminating a great wheeled coach, pulled by four madly galloping black horses. The coach rattled over a mud-rutted stretch of road between rows of bulked, low-crouching trees. Daggered branches, driven by a gusting wind, slashed at the swaying vehicle as it passed beneath them.

A skeletal coachman in greatcoat and top hat was handling the reins, his ragged black scarf streaming behind him. He punished the laboring horses with sharp-cracking cuts from a long whip.

Carmilla gripped my shoulders fiercely with her taloned hands. "He's waiting!" she said—and tossed me upward toward the screen with demonic strength.

I landed heavily on my back on the slimed road, with the chilled rain beating down, instantly soaking my skin and clothing. Stunned, I raised my head to see the coach rapidly bearing down upon me, a dark juggernaut in the rain-lashed night. The massive, foam-flecked horses loomed against the trees, steam pouring from their distended nostrils, eyes rolling in their long skulls.

I threw up both hands in a futile attempt to shield myself from the onrush of their muscled bodies, from the sharp-edged death in their pounding hooves . . .

"Whoa! . . . Whoa there, my beauties!" shouted the bone-white coachman, pulling hard on the reins. The four horses strained back, neighing wildly, as the great coach came to a creaking halt.

A door along the side of the vehicle opened, and from his high perch the coachman beckoned me forward. "Inside. He's inside."

Dazed and uncertain, I got to my feet and pulled myself into the coach. Instantly, the whip cracked and the ponderous vehicle lurched forward. Off balance, I was thrown to the floor. I looked up, unable to make out the dark figure seated across from me. Then a bright bolt of lightning illumined the coach interior and I saw him clearly.

His eyes were dark and sunken, with gray lifeless skin stretched over the thrusting bones of his face. Sections of flesh had rotted away to raw skull—and there was a blackened hole in his left temple.

"Hello, Raymond," said Julian Pascal.

The phone rang, a loud penetrating jangle above the noise of the drumming rain. I scrabbled to answer it, gripped the receiver, and pulled it free of its cradle. My hand was trembling.

"Ray . . ." Erle's concerned voice pulsed over the wire. "Are you *there*, Ray?"

I was sitting up in bed, pressing the phone to my ear, my heart pounding, breathing raggedly, as Cissy stirred into wakefulness beside me.

"I'm here," I said. "Your call brought me out of a nightmare. A real lulu. I'm still shaky."

"News on the Countess," he said. "I left Tomas to watch her place. Right now, I'm at a pay phone on Franklin."

I told Cissy that it was Erle. She nodded, settling back into her pillow.

"What have you got?" I asked Gardner.

"She's set up a meeting with Enright."

"How do you know that?"

"I was close to the house, under a window, while she was having a phone conversation. Heard everything. She used the name 'Merv' so I knew it was our boy. 'I have the rest of the money ready,' she told him. Sounded angry and fed up. She warned him, 'You'd better have it, because I want this to end.' "

"Could be he's been blackmailing her," I said.

"Yeah, that's how I make it," Erle agreed. "Looks like Carmilla is trying to buy whatever was in that package she went after."

"Do you know when they plan to meet?"

"Tonight," said Gardner. "Before three."

"Where?"

"No way of telling. But I heard her say, 'I know the road. I can be there by three.' That's all I've got."

"It's enough," I said. "You head back. I'll pick up Dash and meet you outside her place. I know he'll want to be in on this."

When I put down the receiver Cissy was frowning at me. "I don't like it," she said.

"You don't like what?"

"Whatever it is that you plan to do tonight. I heard you talk about blackmail . . ."

I was sitting on the edge of the bed, pulling on a pair of socks. "The Countess is meeting Enright. It's likely he's been blackmailing her. She's going out to confront him, and I need to be there."

"Why?"

"Because he's the key to everything—including Julian's death."

"You don't know that. There's been no real connection established."

"Not yet," I said. "But Elina is—"

"I don't like it," she interrupted. Her face was pale and I could read the fear in her eyes.

"I'm finding out more all the time. I need to follow this through."

"What was that about a nightmare?"

I told her about the dream as I was getting dressed. When I got to the part about Julian "waiting for me" inside the night coach she looked concerned.

"How did you react to him?"

"I was terrified." I stopped buttoning my shirt and faced her. "And that's damned odd. Why should I fear Julian?"

"You fear what he represented in your dream," she declared.

"And what was that? What did he represent?"

"Death," she said quietly. "He was Death."

"My God!" I sat down on the bed again, emotionally shaken. "What's happening to me?"

"Your subconscious fears are surfacing," she told me. "You're afraid of Merv Enright, of what he might do. That's what your dream meant."

"All right, I admit I'm scared. I'm out of my depth. I'm no ex–Pinkerton detective, I'm an ex–British gentleman. What am I doing chasing after killers?"

"Exactly," nodded Cissy. "So don't go tonight. Let the others handle this. Stay out of it."

"You asked me to find the truth behind Julian's death—and that's all I've been trying to do."

"I also told you I didn't want you hurt. This whole thing is coming down on you—like that coach in your dream." She gripped my arm. "*Listen* to what your subconscious is telling you, Raymio! Don't go any further."

I squeezed her hand, leaned to kiss her gently on those pale, soft lips. "I can't stop now, Cissy."

And I couldn't.

* * *

I arrived with Hammett shortly before 2:00 A.M., pulling the Duesenberg in behind Gardner's parked camper truck. Erle left his vehicle and walked back to ours, opening the rear passenger door and climbing inside. He looked pleased with himself.

"Everything's jake," he said. "She'll have to come out the front and we can tail her from here. Tomas is going to drive the camper back to my house after we leave."

I had a clear view of Carmilla's front gate, a few hundred feet ahead of us down the hill. A streetlight made the black iron gleam.

There was a question I was dying to ask Gardner. "How did you get inside the grounds and under that window without alerting Bruno? He doesn't take kindly to intruders."

"I waited until the house maid took him for a walk," declared Erle. "That's when I went in and managed to overhear her conversation with Enright. My timing was perfect."

I nodded. "Maybe fate is on our side."

"Fate didn't have anything to do with it," growled Hammett. "Erle was just dumb-ass lucky."

"We can follow Enright after they meet and find where he's hiding out," I said.

"What if Carmilla spots us?" asked Gardner.

"She won't," I said. "Her mind will be fully occupied with tonight's action. Why should she suspect anyone of following her?"

"Ray's got it right," said Hammett. "I did a lot of shadowing with the Pinks and I found that people never figure they're being tailed. One guy I was shadowing got lost in the suburbs and *I* had to give him directions so he could get back to the city. If you play it smart, tailing somebody is a cinch."

Gardner checked his watch. "My guess is that the Countess ought to be rolling any time now."

"Did you get some good material for your Jenkins story?" I asked him.

"Yeah, now I know how it feels to be on a stakeout." He grinned. "But there's one part I can't write about."

"What part?"

"The part about having to pee—I mean, *really* having to pee—and not being able to. In my story for Shaw, I can't have Ed Jenkins sitting there with a distended bladder, praying for a chance to pee."

"I thought you'd be able to take care of that sort of thing in your camper truck," I said.

"Not without leaving the gate unwatched."

"Kill the piss talk," said Hammett. "She's coming out."

Lights flared from the driveway. A uniformed maid swung the iron gate wide as Carmilla's long white Cadillac sedan, with her behind the wheel, rolled onto the street, turning left downhill and motoring quietly off into the darkness.

As Mr. Holmes would put it, the game was afoot.

I was correct about the Countess; she was too preoccupied with her upcoming rendezvous to notice my car in her rearview mirror. Nevertheless, I kept well back, giving her plenty of running room as she headed north on Highland Avenue out of Hollywood, then through the Cahuenga Pass toward Ventura Boulevard—the historic El Camino Real—and the foothills of the San Fernando Valley.

We drove in silence for several miles, passing through Valley communities laid out along the boulevard like pearls on a string. Studio City, home of Republic Pictures, the company that had taken over the sprawling Mack Sennett "Keystone Cops" film property; quiet, residential, turn-of-the-century Sherman Oaks; graceful pastoral Encino ("oak" in Spanish), from the name given to the Valley, El Valle de Santa Catalina de Bononia de los Encinos, in 1769 by Gaspar de Portolá's pioneering expedition in honor of Bononia, Portolá's birthplace in Spain, and the Valley's many ancient native trees, some over a thousand years old; and Tarzana, since 1918 the home of Edgar Rice Burroughs, and named for his most famous character.

Finally, still trailing Carmilla, we drove through the foothills at the far western edge of the Valley, ascending the Chalk Hill grade to Girard, an intimate, pleasant little community of tree-covered hills named for its visionary developer, Victor Girard, whose farsighted subdivision plans in the mid-1920s had been disastrously aborted by the Depression. Although the community, with fewer than a hundred residents, is little more than a ghost town these days, it still retains the bucolic charm Girard envisioned in 1924.

Now we were driving through the original Rancho El Escorpion, the fabled land of Father Junípero Serra and his brown-robed Franciscan mission founders, and later the territory of the legendary outlaw Joaquín Murrieta.

The Countess turned south at Canoga Avenue and drove toward the nearby Santa Monica Mountains. Ten miles ahead, the towering purple sierra bounded the Pacific. The road Carmilla had mentioned in her telephone conversation turned out to be Mulholland Drive, named for William Mulholland, the canny engineer who earned enduring gratitude in 1913 by designing an aqueduct system which brought water from the Owens Valley, 250 miles northeast, to the parched desert on which greater Los Angeles is located.

Water in the desert is more valuable than gold. With his innovative system, William Mulholland had made it possible for the sleepy pueblo of Los Angeles to be transformed into a growing major metropolis. Mulholland Drive, looping along the crest of the Santa Monica Mountains, is one of the longest and most dramatically beautiful roadways in the nation, the city's tribute to the man who had assured its future.

We quickly encountered an undeveloped, solitary stretch of Mulholland which was little more than a rutted dirt track. On one side was a wooden sign:

Ungraded Road
DANGER!
CAUTION ADVISED
City of Los Angeles

To me, the warning seemed ominously prophetic. We *were* moving into danger, and caution was most certainly advised.

I followed the white Cad as it negotiated a hard left off the pavement onto pitted gravel. Just before making the turn, I killed my lights. Driving without headlights on such a dangerous stretch was risky business, but I had no choice. Otherwise, Carmilla would have instantly been alerted to our presence.

The road was a wash of charcoal blackness, ridged with dips and potholes. From the dashboard, I adjusted the suspension for rough terrain, a special feature of the Duesenberg which I appreciated. Ahead of us, leading me on: the floating red taillights of the Cadillac, a moving ghost in the night.

"Talk about spooky," muttered Gardner. "This is *real* vampire country!"

"But tonight the blood sucking comes from Enright," added Hammett.

We were a couple of miles beyond the pavement when a pair of headlights flared into life in the near-distance, blinking three times: on-off . . . on-off . . . on-off. The Cadillac responded with the same pattern.

"That's our boy," said Hammett. "Better pull over. We can't chance getting too close."

I eased to the far edge of the road, cutting the engine, and we cranked down the door windows. The night sound of crickets swelled around us. The surrounding mass of heavy chaparral and sage helped shield our car, but a glint of chrome could easily betray us.

The two vehicles rolled slowly toward each other like questing animals, tires grinding against cold gravel, probing the road. Carmilla stopped her car thirty feet short of Enright's truck, their four headlights carving a dusty circle of raw brightness from the shrouding dark.

The Ford's door opened with a squeak of rusted metal and Merv got out, joined by his two beefcakes, Al and Arnie. Elina was nowhere in sight, but I hadn't expected her to be here. The Countess stepped out of the Cad in a long black fur coat, a dark hat pulled low over her face.

I watched Enright through a pair of binoculars as he waved his goons back and walked forward to meet the Countess, both of them chalk white in the powdered cone of headlights.

"Did you bring the cash?" he asked her. His voice was a low rumble, but in the silence of the dark night the words were distinct.

"I said I would, didn't I?" She took a roll of bills from her pocket, holding them out to him. "Now give me what I came for."

Enright accepted the money, flipping through the bills in a quick count. Satisfied, he put the roll into his coat pocket, taking out a cigarette and lighting it.

"Quit stalling, you bastard! Hand it over!" Carmilla's tension-filled voice rang with anger.

"Don't get tough with me," snapped Enright. "I could blow

your frigging head off right here and now, and nobody would ever know who iced you. Yeah . . . and I got half a mind to do it.''

She didn't respond, just stared at him. I could tell from the rigid set of her shoulders that she was afraid he'd carry out the threat.

"Dammit!" whispered Dash. "If he tries anything—"

"He won't," I said. "Merv's got the money. He'll give her what she wants. If he was planning to kill her, he'd have one of his pet apes do it. And he's waved them off.''

When Enright reached into his coat she flinched back. Was he pulling heat? He grinned, removing a package from an inner pocket. "You can be grateful that I'm a man of my word," he said, handing her the package.

Hurriedly, she untied the string and stripped away the white butcher paper.

Erle leaned close: "Can you see what it is?"

I peered through the binoculars. "A gun," I said. "I don't know what make."

"Gimme," said Hammett, taking the binoculars. After an adjustment, he nodded: "Pearl-grip .22-caliber Banker's Special. A lady's piece."

Carmilla was holding the .22 tightly in her hand.

"It's not loaded," declared Enright, "so there's no use pointing it at me."

That was when one of Enright's boys spotted us. Arnie yelled, pointing in our direction: "Somebody's back there!"

Enright cupped a hand to his eyes, squinting past the lights. "It's Chandler!"

Merv jerked a .45 from his belt while his goons ran for weapons in the Ford and got off two rounds before I was able to start the engine. Hammett and Gardner ducked low in the seat.

"Christ!" snarled Dash. "*Move* this thing!"

I hit the throttle and lights, slewing the big Duesenberg around in a churning spin, then straightening out for our run to pavement. By now, Enright's boys had opened up on us and I heard the deadly chatter of a Thompson; bullets clanged against the coachwork.

I floored the pedal as we shot forward, bashing over the road dips. Merv and his men piled into the Ford, blasting off after us.

The gap narrowed as we bounced along the ungraded road; Enright's Ford truck was lighter and faster. We were in serious trouble. Bullets rained around us as the Ford closed to within a few hundred feet. Thankfully, Hammett had brought along his .38, and now he knelt backward on the seat, facing our pursuers, and began firing.

He was good. One of his rounds took out their left headlight and another shattered the Ford's windshield. Enright lost control and the truck slid violently into a stand of boulders flanking the road, tumbleweeds exploding around it.

The chase was over.

NINETEEN

Early the next morning I was outside Carmilla's mansion with my thumb on the gate buzzer. The maid came to answer it, saw who I was, and opened the gate for me. I drove inside, parking under the wide portico at the house entrance. The Vampire Queen was standing at the front door with a drink in her right hand, waiting for me.

"We need to talk," I said.

She nodded. "I've been expecting you. Bruno is locked in the den, so he won't bother us. And the maid is leaving now; I've given her the rest of the day off. We'll be alone in the house."

"Swell," I said.

We went inside to the library. I sat down, refused a drink, and watched the Countess as she freshened her glass of Scotch at the portable bar.

She sat down opposite me on the sofa, placing her glass on the small occasional table at her elbow. "Why did you follow me last night?"

"You're using your right hand," I said. "I thought you were left-handed."

"Nerve damage," she declared. "I can hardly close my fingers anymore. The doctor says it's permanent; I must learn to use my right hand for everything. Very troublesome. But allow me to repeat my question, Mr. Chandler. Why did you follow me last night?''

"I was curious.''

"And you saw what Enright gave me?''

"Yes . . . a gun.''

"*This* gun!'' She stood up, the pearl-handled .22 in her right hand. It was pointed at me, and this time I knew it was loaded. "I can't let you spoil everything now.''

I tried to stay calm, but my heart was doing cartwheels. "I don't think you want another dead body on your hands.''

"So you've figured it out?''

"Just before I drove over here this morning I called Captain McQuillan. He checked the DuPlaine file and verified the fact that the fatal bullet came from a .22-caliber weapon. My guess is that you were with DuPlaine that night and that the .22 you're holding is the gun that killed him.''

She slumped down in an antique velvet chair, lowering the weapon. Her eyes were haunted with dark memories. "Yes, this *is* the gun . . . and yes, I did shoot David with it.''

"And when Merv Enright got his hands on it, he came up with the bright idea of blackmailing you. Threatened to turn it over to the law if you didn't kick through.''

She nodded, easing back in the chair. "I used this gun in all of my Dragon films. The police would have no trouble establishing that it's mine. Which is why I couldn't allow it to fall into their possession. And yet . . . I don't want to kill you, Mr. Chandler. I want no more killing.'' Her head was down and she looked weary and defeated.

My heartbeat slowly returned to normal. There was still a lot to be said and I felt she was ready to say it.

"When you got fed up paying, you hired me to find Enright so

201

you could try to reclaim the gun. But that didn't work out."

"Merv knew I was becoming desperate," she said, her voice dulled and mechanical. "He agreed to a return last night—for a final payment."

"How did he get your gun in the first place?"

"My sister was there with me that night. She saw me kill David. Elina promised that she'd get rid of the gun for me."

"Then why didn't she?"

"I don't *know* why. I do know that she was terribly frightened and upset. Somehow Enright discovered the gun. He needed money—"

"And he knew you could supply it?"

She nodded. "Elina admitted to me that she stays with Merv only out of fear. He beats her . . . controls her completely. She has no life of her own. In reality, Elina is Merv Enright's prisoner."

"So what you told me about talking to her only once in the past three years . . . that was another lie."

"Yes. We've had several phone conversations. I kept trying to find out where she was, but she'd never tell me."

"I want to know about the night of the murder. Everything you can remember."

"Will you turn me over to the police?"

"What I will or won't do is not the issue right now." I looked steadily at her. "Tell me about DuPlaine's murder."

She stood up again and began pacing the room the way a trapped panther paces a cage.

"David and I had been fighting that evening—saying really bitter, horrible things to each other."

"What was the fight about?"

"David was involved with another woman. I don't know who she was, but I knew the situation existed, and I was quite jealous and angry." She hesitated, drawing in several deep breaths. "We were both drinking that night, I more than David. I was trying to numb the ghastly pain. I loved him very much, you know."

"Okay," I said, "so you had this gun. Did you have it with you that night in DuPlaine's house?"

"Not at first. It was still in the glove box of the Cadillac."

"When did you bring it into the house?"

"I don't remember exactly. There are many things about that night that I don't remember." She stopped; her hands were trembling. "I need to finish my drink."

I handed the Scotch to her and she downed it hurriedly. It seemed to drain some of the tension from her body. She sat down on the sofa again, fixing her eyes on mine.

"After I . . . shot David . . . I . . . I blacked out—and when I came to, I was still holding the gun. Elina had seen it all, and she was terrified."

"And so the two of you faked a robbery?"

"Yes. We broke the sunroom window from the garden side and took some silver . . . bowls, a dinner set . . . to make it seem as if a thief had been there."

"And you got out before the police arrived?"

"Yes."

"And Elina took the silver away?"

"Yes. Sometime later, Enright pawned it. But you already know that."

"What else do you remember?"

She drew in another deep breath. Her voice was a low, pained mumble. "I remember leaving David lying there on his back in the living room. Blood had pooled around his body. There was so much . . . so *much* blood . . ." She lowered her head, tears on her cheeks. "And the awful part is . . . I loved him . . . I really loved him."

I walked over to a cedarwood bookcase, running my thumb along its glass facing. "I've got to tell the police about this. You've just confessed to a murder, and if I don't report it, I'm an accessory."

Carmilla raised her head like a frightened animal. "I'll tell them everything I told you, on my own, as a voluntary act."

"You mean, you want to go down to the station with me and—"

"No, no!" There was desperation in her tone. "Please, Mr. Chandler, grant me the dignity of doing this alone. Give me twenty-four hours. To get my legal papers in order, to take care of personal matters."

"How do I know you won't try to run? Or maybe it's suicide you're thinking about."

The Countess shook her head violently. "I *swear* to you that within twenty-four hours I'll turn myself in to the police." She was literally begging me. "Please, trust me, Mr. Chandler!"

I was standing above her. "You're not an easy woman to trust. You've lied to me before."

"I'm not lying to you now," she declared. "I *want* to get all this over, to pay for what I did to David. I've been in hell since that night. I want to tell the truth."

"I'll probably damn well regret this."

She brightened instantly. "Then you'll *do* it—you'll give me some time."

"Tomorrow morning I'll be calling McQuillan to make certain you've turned yourself in. If you haven't—"

"I will, I will!"

"If you haven't," I continued, "I'll personally hunt you down no matter how long it takes. And when I find you—"

"You won't need to hunt me down," she said. "I'll honor my word. You'll see."

"Twenty-four hours," I said.

That's when I left her, thinking: Chandler, you're a gullible fool to be walking away from this.

The trouble was—I *believed* her.

I was on my way home, halfway to Culver City, and wondering how I was going to explain all this to Cissy, when a cabdriver began blowing his horn behind me.

Had I inadvertently cut in front of him? Or was I blocking his lane? My mind *was* distracted, but I was certain this had not affected my driving. Maybe the guy was some kind of malcontent who was sore at everybody and everything. Driving a taxi in L.A. can do that to you.

I edged over to the right, sticking my left hand out the window to wave him past, but he didn't go around me. He rode my rear bumper, still tooting. I was beginning to get angry when I realized why he was pulling this act. He was gesturing toward the curb; he wanted me to stop.

I eased to the curbing, braked the Duesenberg, and waited. Sure enough, he pulled up behind me and stopped the cab. The rear door opened and a passenger got out, paid him, then walked briskly toward me.

A woman.

Elina.

I was stunned. Her sudden appearance was a complete surprise. What did this mean? Why had she flagged me down?

"Mr. Chandler?" Her voice was strained. She stood on the walk, gripping the doorframe. Same long blonde hair. Same heart-shaped face, her eyes obscured by dark sunglasses. She was in a beige afternoon dress that accented her trim figure, but her hair had been combed carelessly and she had not applied makeup. She looked disturbed.

"I'm Chandler."

"I didn't think anyone else would be driving a car like this," she said. "May I get in?"

I leaned across to open the door for her and she slipped into the seat next to me. "Is there someplace quiet where we can talk?" Her voice was tense.

"There's a little restaurant about three blocks from here, Chez Pierre. Nothing going on there this time of day."

"Fine," she said as I angled the Duesenberg back into the traffic flow. "Merv told me about you . . . what you look like . . . about this car." She hesitated, obviously uncomfortable. "He said he tried to kill you."

I nodded. "Him and his two goons. Did you know about the meeting last night?"

"Yes."

"Well, they put several bullet holes in my coachwork. Being shot at is damned frightening. Your boyfriend is a public menace!"

"He's no friend of mine, he's a monster!" she said tightly. "And I'm not surprised he tried to kill you. He's capable of anything."

We reached Pierre's, a brick building styled to look like a Parisian brasserie, with a blinking neon cocktail glass in the street window. I parked and we went inside.

Nobody was in the bar, just the lantern-jawed guy tending it and a bored-looking waitress with skinny legs dressed in a tight skirt, net stockings, and black high heels that would have looked a lot more appropriate on a French streetwalker.

We settled into a corner booth as the waitress walked over, swinging her hips.

"Hi, I'm Michelle. What can I get you?"

"Pernod," I said. Elina ordered the same.

"Well . . . ," I said, facing her across the table. "Here I've been

206

trying to figure out how to find you, and instead you find *me*."

"You're the only person I can turn to." She tried out a faint smile. "Guess you're what I could call my 'last hope.' Dramatic, huh?"

"Very," I said. "But before we get into why you're here, let me ask about someone who was once very close to you."

"Who?"

"Julian Pascal. What do you know about his death?"

"Julian . . . *dead?*" She seemed genuinely shocked.

"His body was found in a Chinese cemetery in East Los Angeles," I said. "Apparent suicide. Only it probably wasn't. It was probably murder."

She looked shaken, lacing her fingers tightly together on the table. "I haven't . . . hadn't . . . seen Julian for a very long while."

"Your sister told me that the two of you once were—"

"That was ages ago—before I got involved with Merv. Julian and I . . . we lost contact. I'm very sorry to hear he's dead. He was a decent man."

As the waitress brought us our drinks Elina removed her sunglasses to dab at her eyes with a tiny lace handkerchief. The area around her right eye was purple.

"How did you get *that?*" I asked.

"Merv hit me," she said tightly. "It's why I've come to you."

"Your sister told me that he beats you . . . that you're afraid of him."

"I'm *terrified* of him," she declared. "He broke my nose last summer. Once he kicked me so hard he cracked two of my ribs. That time I had to go to the hospital. I told the doctor that I'd fallen on some stairs. I'm not sure he believed me, but he taped me up."

"Where is Enright now?"

"He's got some kind of crooked deal set up out in the desert near Indio. I don't know the details."

"Why didn't he take you along?"

"He would have—just to keep me under his thumb—but I pretended to have the flu, so he let me stay. We're living in a house on Ridgecrest. Belongs to a pal of Merv's who's in Europe." She pushed back a loose strand of hair.

"How did you find me?"

"I phoned my sister. She gave me your address in Culver City. That's where I was going in the cab. I phoned when Merv was gone. He doesn't want me contacting Carmilla. He said that if he ever found out I'd talked to her, or tried to see her, he'd make me 'real sorry.' And I've learned to take his threats very seriously."

"Did she tell you that she had made a full confession to me—about killing David DuPlaine?"

"Yes. She said you gave her twenty-four hours to turn herself in to the police. And I want to thank you for that."

"Tell me everything that happened on the night your sister shot DuPlaine."

She looked down at her hands, began tracing nervous circles on the tabletop with an index finger. "There was a movie premiere in Hollywood that night—Gary Cooper starred in it—and I remember Coop was there and said hello to my sister. Carmilla had a silver flask full of Scotch in her purse and kept nipping all through the picture. On the way back she insisted that we stop at David's place."

"You knew about her affair with him, right?"

"Of course. She always confided in me in those days."

"I want to get the timeline straight in my mind," I said. "You'd given up your screen career by then, but you hadn't yet met Enright."

"I'd *met* him, but I was still living with Carmilla."

"Why didn't DuPlaine attend the premiere with her that night? They found a ticket in his coat."

208

"He told Carmilla that he had an urgent business appointment. Originally, we were to meet at the premiere."

"Was he telling her the truth about the appointment?"

"At first she thought he was, but then at the premiere she began brooding about it. The more she drank the more convinced she became that he was with another woman."

"And *was* he?"

"Not that night, but he *had* been having an outside affair. He wasn't very discreet about it, and Carmilla found out. She was very jealous."

"So she insisted on going over to DuPlaine's house after the premiere?"

"Yes. And by then she was really boiled. When we got to David's he was alone, but that didn't satisfy her. She began screaming at him about what a cruel bastard he was for cheating on her, and how she'd been totally faithful to him. I tried to get her to leave, but she wouldn't. The two of them just kept at each other. It turned into a real shouting match."

"How about DuPlaine—how much did he have to drink?"

"I don't know, but he wasn't anywhere near as drunk as she was."

"Then what happened?"

"She staggered out to the Cadillac and got her .22 from the glove compartment. When she came back into the house she had it in her hand."

"Did DuPlaine try to take the gun away from her?"

"He sure did. They struggled over it until . . ." Her eyes darkened. "I watched her shoot him. A single bullet in the chest. Then she blacked out with the gun still in her hand."

"Had she suffered prior blackouts from drinking?"

"Many times. Alcohol often affects my sister this way. A *lot* of it, I mean."

"How long did she remain unconscious that night?"

"About half an hour . . . maybe forty minutes. I was in a panic. When Carmilla came to her senses, I told her we had to fake a robbery to throw off the police. That's when we broke the sun-room window and took the silver. She gave me the gun, and I promised her I'd get rid of it."

"Why didn't you?"

"I don't honestly know. I *meant* to, but . . . after that awful night . . . I just couldn't bring myself to deal with it."

"How did Enright get the gun?"

"He found out that I had it and he . . . just took it."

"And you let him?"

"I had no idea what he planned to do with it." She looked steadily at me. "You must understand, Mr. Chandler, that at the time, I *thought* I loved him. Merv seemed to understand what I'd been through—and he swore he'd get rid of the gun for me. Instead, he used it to blackmail my sister."

"What I can't understand is why you didn't leave him."

"I was afraid to. Merv said if I ever left him, he'd kill me. As you have learned, he's a very violent man."

I couldn't argue with that. Once a vulnerable woman gets caught in the grip of a psychotic individual like Enright it's extremely difficult for her to break off the relationship.

"When do you expect him back in town?"

"Late tonight."

"What about his two boys, Al and Arnie? Both still with him?"

"No. They took off for San Francisco last night, after that road thing. Afraid of being arrested."

"Okay," I said. "There's a homicide captain I know who'll be real happy to nail a creep like Enright. And there's plenty to charge him with: blackmail, assault, attempted murder. They'll put him where he won't bother you or anybody else."

She shook her head. "We can't do it that way. If I'm there

210

when the police come for Merv, I'll be implicated as an accomplice. And I'll end up in jail."

"Then don't go back. Just give me the address and I'll have him picked up tonight."

"If I'm not there, he'll know something is wrong. He could get away. I want *you* to do this. You and your two friends. Come to the house and I'll signal from the window that Merv is inside. You come in and take him. Then, after I'm gone, you can call in the cops."

"Enright is bound to involve you. You'll be a fugitive."

"They won't find me. I'll leave California and start a new life somewhere else under another name. It's the only chance I've got."

"What about your sister? You'll be running out on her."

"I know, and I feel awful about Carmilla. But she *did* kill David. That's something she has to face alone."

I thought about everything she'd said. "Enright is a dangerous man. Carries a .45 in his belt."

"Your friend has a gun," she said. "Merv told me about how he shot out his windshield. Believe me, it won't be that difficult. I'll leave the front door open and signal you when to come in. And I'll make sure he's not carrying the automatic. You'll be able to surprise him."

When I continued to look dubious she said: "I won't give you the address until I have your word you'll do it my way."

I nodded, knowing this was our only chance to nail Enright. "Okay, you've got my word. Now . . . where's the house?"

And she told me.

When I arrived home Cissy met me at the door, looking agitated. She was holding a letter in her hand.

"You'd better read this, Raymio," she said. "It was stuck in the bundle of letters you took from Julian's apartment. The ones

I wrote to him. I've been so depressed over Julian that I just couldn't bear to look at them—until now. This is a rough draft of a letter he apparently intended to send to me, and it was written the same week he died."

I sat down and read it. Julian was confiding in Cissy, meandering on paper the same way he would have spoken to her had they been having a conversation. He was obviously upset, and—quite uncharacteristically, given his meticulous nature—the pages showed several cross-outs, false starts, and hesitations.

"I think this letter might be directly related to Julian's death," Cissy declared. "He was murdered before he could send it."

I nodded, shocked at the contents.

"Is there enough here to go to the police?" she asked.

"No. What Julian wrote wouldn't mean anything to them. But I want to hang on to this." I folded the pages and slipped them into my coat.

Julian's letter had given me a great deal to think about.

TWENTY

Ridgecrest Road twists up from Laurel Canyon, snaking along the brushy mountain ridge above the San Fernando Valley in a series of shallow dips and sharp-angled turns. This was a warm, windless spring night, with a sky full of crushed diamonds above and the firefly lights of the Valley spread out below in undulating waves.

Hammett and Gardner were with me in the Duesenberg, not saying much, staring at the road that unwound ahead of us, looking the way soldiers look before a battle. Dash carried the only weapon, his .38 in a clamshell belt holster with extra rounds in his coat pocket.

Cissy was furious with me for going on this wild excursion, and when I left the house that night she refused to say good-bye. I couldn't blame her for feeling the way she did. Indeed, this was a prime example of a "fool's errand."

"Once we arrive," said Erle, "how will we know when it's safe to go in?"

"With Enright there, it *won't* be," I told him. "But Elina will signal us at eleven. If he's inside, and suspects nothing, she'll lower the shade on the porch window. That will be our signal to move. And she'll have the front door unlatched."

"I just hope she separates him from that .45 of his," Dash said. "I don't like ducking bullets."

Erle glanced at him curiously. "When you were with Pinkerton, did you ever get shot?"

"Sure," replied Hammett.

"More than once?"

"Shut up, Erle," I snapped. "You're getting on my nerves. Drop the subject."

"Well, I just wondered." Gardner shrugged, lapsing into silence.

Another mile and we reached a wooden sign:

WARNING!
ROAD ENDS

No Maintenance Beyond This Point
City of Los Angeles

"The house is just beyond the end of Ridgecrest," I said. "On top of the hill."

Now it was visible: a tile-roofed, single-story Territorial-style adobe with an outside patio deck, a stone porch, and a two-car garage—an impressive move up from the trailer in Venice.

"We walk from here," I said, stopping the car in a patch of deep road shadow. The crickets were in full harmony and the intense night smell of sagebrush was strong in our nostrils. The palms of my hands were sweating; I didn't fancy the job we were setting out to accomplish.

The climb was a steep one, and we were out of breath at the top. Across a wide expanse of heavy brush, the lights of the house shone in the darkness.

We cautiously made our way around the side yard until we

had a clear view of the porch. Lights were on in the living room and the shade was still up.

Dash checked his watch. "It's five to eleven."

That's when we heard Elina scream—a sound as clear in the still night air as a pistol shot.

We sprinted for the porch, Hammett leading, the .38 in his hand. The front door was locked.

"I'm going in," Dash said. "Stay here."

Another scream.

Hammett made a headlong dive through the front window in a splintering shower of glass and wood fragments.

I braced myself for gunfire, but it never came.

Within moments, Dash was on the porch. "She's locked in the bathroom," he said. "Enright is gone."

We had to break down the bathroom door to reach Elina. She'd been bound and gagged, but had managed to struggle free of the ropes and pull the gag from her mouth. That's when she'd started to scream. Her print dress was ripped at one shoulder and she was barefoot. Her eyes were wild.

"Where's Enright?" Dash asked her.

"Out there," she gasped, pointing. "On the deck."

He was there all right—and he was very dead.

His body lay face down on the redwood planking in a square of yellow light from the window. Blood had leaked through the deck cracks, but the flow had ceased; his heart was no longer pumping.

We left Enright. There were questions to ask. A lot of questions.

I walked up to Elina. "Who killed him?"

She was huddled on the living room couch, arms hugging her chest, her face ashen, rocking back and forth like a frightened child. She didn't answer me the first time, so I repeated my question. It was tough on her; she was obviously in a state of shock, but before the cops were called in we had to find out what happened.

"Who killed Enright?"

Elina raised her head slowly, staring at me. "She did."

"She?"

"My sister. With the same gun . . . came here earlier tonight . . . maybe an hour ago . . . crazy drunk. She called Merv a 'blackmailing son of a bitch' and shot him. Then she tied me up and locked me in the bathroom so I couldn't stop her."

"Stop her from what?" asked Erle.

"From killing herself," murmured Elina in a broken voice. "She said she was going to go back home and . . . and end everything."

"We'd better get over there," said Hammett.

"I'll call McQuillan," I said. "Have him send the meat wagon for Enright. Then he can coordinate with us at Carmilla's place."

"Nix on that," snapped Hammett. "It takes a while to work up enough nerve to kill yourself. Carmilla's probably sitting there right now with the .22 in her hand, thinking about using it one more time. A bunch of cops charging in will be all it takes to push her over the edge. We need to handle this ourselves."

"He's right," agreed Elina. "There's still a chance we can save her."

I phoned McQuillan at his home, waking him. I gave him the Ridgecrest address, told him that a dead man was waiting for him, and hung up before he could ask any questions.

Then the four of us headed for my car.

I'm no racing driver, but I drove like Barney Oldfield on that run into Hollywood. Every minute counted. I kept a sharp eye out for patrol cars, but luckily didn't see any—which allowed me to keep the Duesenberg moving along at a fast clip.

Hammett already had the passenger door open as I slammed

to a stop in front of Carmilla's mansion. He leaped for the gate, found it unlocked, and threw it wide. "Go!" he said, jumping on the running board.

I rolled up to the main entrance and we all piled out. There was no trace of Bruno. Maybe he was locked up with the Countess. But he sure wasn't barking. The house was silent, and as black as an inkwell.

"Don't turn on the lights," Hammett warned. "We don't want her to know we're here." To me: "Is there a flashlight in the Duesie?"

"Yeah. Glove box."

"I'll get it," said Erle.

"Dear God, I hope we're in time," breathed Elina. "Do you think she's already—"

Hammett gripped her shoulders; his tone was commanding. "You know the house. Where would she be? Where do we look?"

"We could try the projection room," Elina said, "where she runs her films and keeps all her posters and scrapbooks."

"That's where she took me the first night I was here," I said. "She called it her 'Room of Life.'"

"Where the hell's Erle?" Hammett growled. "We can't move without a light."

Gardner arrived a few seconds later with my metal flash. Its strong beam sliced through the darkness.

"Okay," said Hammett to Elina. "Take us to the projection room. And make it fast."

When we arrived there, pausing in the hallway in front of the closed door, we heard a whirring sound from inside.

The door was unlocked, and we entered the room.

The sound emanated from Carmilla's film projector. On the glowing square of screen, draped in her long black cape, she was rising from her coffin, vampire fangs gleaming in the moonlight,

217

her face transfixed with a savage blood hunger.

I whipped the beam around the room—and we found the real Carmilla. She was seated in a deep velour armchair facing her own flickering screen image, her head resting against the cushioned chairback. She didn't respond to our entry or to the beam of light illuminating her.

There was a single dark powder-burned hole in her forehead.

Bruno lay dead beside her. Carmilla's left hand was in her lap, the fingers curled loosely around the gun that had killed her, the .22 pearl-grip.

"Looks like we're a little late," said Hammett.

Elina turned away, sobbing, as Erle put a comforting arm around her. I stopped the projector and snapped on the lights as Gardner helped Elina to a chair.

"Why?" she moaned. "Why did she have to kill herself?"

"She didn't," I said flatly. "This is no suicide."

"What?" Elina blinked at me.

"The gun," I said. "It's in her left hand."

Elina shook her head, confused. "But my sister was left-handed."

"Normally, yes, but she recently suffered permanent nerve damage. The last time I saw her she talked about it . . . about how she couldn't close the fingers on her left hand anymore and how it was necessary for her to learn to do everything with her right." I paused. "The killer who tried to make this look like suicide didn't know about the nerve damage."

"She was lying to you," said Elina. "When she came over to-night to kill Merv she had the gun in her left hand. There was no indication that she couldn't use that hand. I don't think there's any question about the fact that she shot herself. This *is* suicide, Mr. Chandler."

"Well, I'll admit you know a lot about suicide. You staged Julian's beautifully."

She was suddenly shrill: "Are you saying that *I* killed Julian?"

"That's right. And I'm also saying that you killed David Du-Plaine and your puppet boyfriend, Merv Enright."

Hammett and Gardner were staring at me; this was the last thing they'd expected to hear.

"Now I can see why you write detective stories," said Elina coldly. "It's because you have such a vivid imagination. How could I kill anyone when I was locked in the bathroom?"

"You faked it," I said, "just the way you gave yourself that black eye, pretending that Merv had done it."

She glared at me, saying nothing.

"Let's just run through tonight's activities," I said, "starting with a visit to your sister here at her home. She trusted you completely, so it was a cinch to set up this little scene . . . get her watching one of her vampire films, obtain the .22, walk up to her in the dark, and shoot her in the forehead, close enough to leave powder burns."

"So you're saying I *put* the gun in her hand?"

"Not right away, you didn't. First you needed it to kill Enright so the bullets would match. You went to Ridgecrest, shot him, *then* drove back here and placed the .22 in Carmilla's left hand."

"So how, in this preposterous murder fantasy of yours, could I end up in a *locked* bathroom, tied and gagged?"

"You never were."

"Never in the bathroom! But you *found* me there. You had to break down the door!"

"I mean that you were never tied or gagged. After killing Carmilla, you drove back to Ridgecrest and entered the bathroom, locking it from the inside. There's a small window in there, and you could have opened the window and thrown the key out. I'm sure the cops will find it in the bushes when they know where to look."

"What about the rope and the gag?" asked Gardner. "How could she tie and gag herself?"

"She carried a rope in with her, along with the gag. Left 'em on the floor to make it look as if she'd struggled free. Then, when she knew we could hear her, she started screaming."

"Were you onto her before we came here?" asked Hammett.

"No, not before tonight. I bought her story about being beaten by Enright and wanting to get away for a chance at a new life."

"So it was the gun in Carmilla's left hand that tipped you?" asked Gardner.

"Along with *this*," I said, taking the folded sheets of paper from my coat. "A letter from Julian Pascal to my wife."

I turned to face Elina. "It was written the same week Julian died, just after you went to see him."

"What Julian and I had was ancient history. We'd been out of touch for years. Why would I want to see him?"

"To take advantage of his good nature, his sense of fairness. You wanted to use him. But you found out that he knew about your affair with David DuPlaine."

"That's a lie! I was never sexually involved with David!"

Ignoring her outburst, I went on: "The blackmail money from your sister would dry up eventually, so you went to see your old lover and asked him to use his influence to help you get back into acting. Julian had the connections, and you told him that he 'owed you' based on your past relationship, that he had a 'moral obligation' to help an old flame. But he felt you didn't deserve his help, that you'd double-crossed your own sister when you got sexually involved with her lover. You were shocked that DuPlaine had told Julian about your affair."

"Lies! All lies!" Her face was tense, eyes heated.

"Suddenly you were worried about Julian. Until then, he hadn't told Carmilla that you were the other woman in David's life, and she had never suspected it—but now that you had resurfaced, you were afraid that Julian might go to her and tell her the truth about you and David. You knew how jealous she was, and that she'd never forgive you for betraying her with Duplaine. You'd be cut out of her will—and you couldn't let that happen. Julian had to be shut up."

"That letter's an obvious fake," she declared. "Nothing in it is true."

"So you came up with the ritual Chinese suicide idea," I continued. "But, by then, Julian had written this letter to my wife, telling her that he was in a moral dilemma. Should he help you get back into the industry out of past loyalty? Was he being too judgmental about your relationship with DuPlaine? Of course, you killed him before he could mail the letter." I gave her a cold smile. "They say that the first murder is always the toughest. After killing DuPlaine, I'll bet Julian was easy for you."

"But Carmilla shot David!" Elina protested. "She admitted it to you."

"Sure, she admitted it—*after* you successfully tricked her into believing she'd killed him."

Hammett looked doubtful. "How do you know that Ray?" he asked. "You told us that Carmilla was in a jealous rage that night and that she'd been fighting bitterly with DuPlaine."

"True enough," I said. "But Elina's turning out to be the other woman alters the equation. Carmilla didn't remember shooting DuPlaine. She went into a drunken blackout, and when she came out of it, the gun was in her hand. Elina told her she'd *seen* the shooting."

"But I did! It was Carmilla!" Elina's face was red with anger and indignation.

I continued speaking to Hammett: "Putting everything together, it's now obvious that Elina shot DuPlaine in order to set up her sister for blackmail. After Elina's film career ended, the only money she had access to was Carmilla's. Merv Enright was an ideal patsy: a bully on the outside, but obviously spineless inside and someone she could easily manipulate." I glared at Elina. "It was perfect for you. You could play Merv's victim, when actually you were in full charge from the beginning."

"Why would I want to kill my own sister?"

"Because of the will. Obviously, Carmilla named you as the principal beneficiary. She told me that there were no other relatives left in the family. You'd get it all, her estate, bank accounts, stocks, investments—a nice little haul."

"Since you're so inventive, Mr. Chandler, just how did I kill Julian Pascal?"

"My guess is that when you made *The Dragon's Daughter*, you got interested in Chinese culture. That's not unusual; many actors become personally interested in the milieus surrounding their roles. So you learned enough to be able to rig Julian's death to look like a ritual Chinese suicide—*after* you planted that Chinese book in his apartment. It never belonged to Julian. The shop owner who sold it told me that it had been bought by a white woman."

"Good luck in trying to prove any of this ridiculous nonsense in court," Elina said in a mocking tone. "I'll walk, Mr. Chandler—and then I'll sue you blind for slander and defamation of character!"

"No, you won't," I said, smiling tightly. "Your prints are all over the gun. When you put it into Carmilla's hand, you weren't able to close her fingers around it."

Elina lunged to her feet, darted across the room, and snatched the .22 out of her dead sister's hand. She swung toward me, the gun leveled. "Now, you smart-assed son of a bitch, I'm going to give you what I gave all of them!"

Hammett's .38 roared.

His bullet struck Elina's gun arm and she dropped the .22,

screeching in pain. Blood spurted from the wound as she fell to one knee, gripping her shattered elbow.

Dash carefully picked up the .22, slipping it into his coat pocket. "How did you know her prints were on the gun?"

"I didn't. She could have worn gloves or wiped off the gun before she put it in Camilla's hand, but it was worth a bluff. And it got results."

"It almost got you *killed*," said Gardner.

I took in a deep breath, feeling very shaky. Erle was right about how close I'd come to dying. A sobering realization. I sat down in a chair, my legs suddenly weak. My palms were sweating again.

"She was right about proof," said Hammett. "Until she went for the gun, your case was pretty thin."

"You gonna call McQuillan?" Gardner asked.

"Yeah," I said, taking another deep breath, "I'm gonna call McQuillan."

And I did.

TWENTY-ONE

Another burial.

Another marble orchard.

Black skies. Heavy rain. Perfect weather for interring a vampire. Inside the coffin, she was draped in her long black cape, the one she'd first worn in *The Blood Countess*. It had been my idea, to bury her in the cape. Appropriate, I felt. A bit of irony she'd appreciate. Vampire Queen Buried in Batcape. The papers loved it.

Of course, she was never the Vampire Queen. Not really. She was just a desperately unhappy woman from Newark, New Jersey, named Letty Knibbs, living alone, betrayed by the man she loved, victimized and murdered by her ruthless sister.

But she would be remembered. Her fans would keep her memory alive. Her motion pictures would continue to be shown. Film historians would write books about her, analyze her brooding cinema appeal, dissect her work, and nurture her legend. Chaney . . . Karloff . . . Lugosi . . . Blastok. Carmilla had earned her place in the pantheon of terror.

She would have been flattered at the turnout for her burial. Hundreds of fans crowded the cemetery, shivering under open umbrellas in the chilled downslash of rain, eager for a final encounter with their dark idol.

Studio people had also gathered here, producers and writers and technicians who had worked with her in the plush years of her screen career. No family members, of course, beyond Jack Snowden, her ex-husband. No blood kin. Alone into the cold earth.

Alone.

Cissy and I had helped arrange the burial; I felt obligated to help. Somehow, despite the brief time I had known her, I felt a painful degree of sadness at Carmilla's passing.

Buddy and Margaret were here, standing together in honor of a woman they'd never known. Hammett was here, of course, and Gardner. In neatly pressed dark suits. Paying their final respects.

The minister droned on as ministers do, but I wasn't listening. I was thinking of Carmilla in her prime, tall and regal and commanding on the screen, taking joy in her performance, her black cape unfolding like the wings of night, eyes shining with triumph.

In an odd, tragic way, she had achieved her ultimate dream— to transcend her mortal flesh, to be of the Undead.

Now, because of her unique talent, the Vampire Queen would live forever.

AFTERWORD

It is essential for readers to understand a key element in my Black Mask Boys series. These books are novelistic case reports, each being filed first-person, book to book, by Hammett, Chandler, or Gardner. When I had Dashiell Hammett narrate *The Black Mask Murders*, there was no pretense that he was writing another *Maltese Falcon*; he was simply reporting what had happened in the case of the missing Cat's Eye.

In *The Marble Orchard*, Chandler is not writing a Philip Marlowe novel, he is recounting his experiences in relation to the death of Julian Pascal and the events that followed it. And in the third book of my series, when I have Erle Stanley Gardner narrate *Sharks Never Sleep*, he will not be dictating a Perry Mason novel, he will be filing a firsthand case report.

What I am doing with these books is rooted in and inspired by the real-life agency reports filed by Hammett when he worked on and off as a Pinkerton detective from 1915 into 1922. (He once claimed these case reports taught him how to write.) My reports are, of course, much more elaborate and are presented within a novelistic framework for dramatic effect—but they are *reports* nonetheless.

I make no claim to have reproduced, exactly and precisely, the writing style of each author. Since, in my books, these writers are "talking on paper," their narrative voices are modified. I *have* tried to maintain the individual flavor of each author's style within this report mode; certainly, the Chandler of *The Marble Orchard* differs considerably from the Hammett of *The Black Mask Murders*.

Chandler is much more loquacious and self-reflective, and though he is definitely tough-minded, he is not nearly as tough as Hammett in a physical sense. He was, after all, raised to be a British gentleman. His habitual perceptions are unique: He notices and describes a character's clothing and appearance in greater detail, is given to outrageous similes on occasion (more on these later), and is keenly attuned to locale and landscape (flowers, trees, furniture, architecture, geography, etc.).

Chandler's classical education in England stands in direct contrast to that of Hammett, who was self-taught, after being forced to leave school at fourteen. The cop/gangster argot so natural to Hammett's world was a foreign language to Chandler; he reproduced it with fascination, not familiarity. Chandler *wrote* about the mean streets; Hammett had *walked* them.

Of course, the murder cases they are involved in throughout this series are entirely fictional. But there *is* reality here; the Hollywood background of the 1930s is as factual as I can make it, and I use many actual personalities, including legendary film stars, to flesh out the era.

Julian Pascal was the real ex-husband of Cissy Chandler and his early background is authentic. I have no idea when and how he died, but he certainly was not murdered in a Chinese cemetery.

Cissy, herself, is something of a mystery woman. In all of the Chandler material I've read, there are very few references to her (beyond Chandler's own letters). I could find no personal memoirs by others relating to Cissy and her daily life with Chandler. Yet I feel that my portrait of her in this book is true to Cissy's spirit and character. She *was* the abiding love of Chandler's life. After her death he self-destructed, even attempted suicide.

Hammett's actual chauffeur was a "Negro" named Jones (reflective of the period, his first name is unrecorded). In this series, he has been fictionalized into Haitian immigrant Leonce "Buddy" Desvarieux. The character of Margaret Stetler is invented, but the embryonic relationship between Margaret and Buddy—as well as the interaction of these two people with the other characters in the novel—illuminates a vital, sparsely recorded, and heretofore largely invisible part of 1930s American life: the black experience.

The name of the western San Fernando Valley community of Girard was changed to Woodland Hills in 1941, five years after the events in this novel—and several years before my wife's parents moved there (from near the Los Angeles Coliseum and U.S.C.) to establish their family residence, thus making Woodland Hills my wife's "hometown."

Legally, there is no such place as Woodland Hills; it is simply one of the several dozen communities which, grouped together, constitute the vast and highly varied geographical area within the corporate limits of the City of Los Angeles. Legalities aside, the various communities within the city have individual, well-defined identities recognized by all Angelenos (and in the case of Hollywood, by the world), and my wife is proud to be the daughter of one of the first post–World War II "pioneering" families in Woodland Hills.

The personal history I have attached to each of my three protagonists, Hammett, Chandler, and Gardner, is based entirely on historical fact. As for dialogue, I have them say what they very well *might* have said within the fictional situations I provide. In other words, I "play fair"—which is the job and responsibility of every historical novelist. My historical approach may be lighter, faster, funnier, but it is no less relevant.

I believe that *The Marble Orchard* is fundamentally a more serious novel than *The Black Mask Murders*, but that's because Chandler was essentially a more serious man than was Hammett; certainly he was much more open in an emotional sense. Hammett always played his cards very close to the vest; he mistrusted emotionalism and valued precise objectivity.

There is also a basic difference in *attitude* between the two: Hammett was frittering away his life and career in the 1930s; Chandler, on the other hand, was *building* his life and career. I think this is reflected in the content of my two books. Despite Hammett's on-again, off-again love/hate relationship with Lillian Hellman, he had no single companion, no Cissy, in his life. He was, in effect, drifting without an emotional rudder.

As regards Chandler's vaunted style, the reader may be disappointed to find that there are very few really outrageous similes in *The Marble Orchard*. Surprisingly, as I discovered in researching his work, Chandler used these *only* in his novels—the first of which was published three years after the events depicted in my book. A careful reading of his shorter 1930s fiction will prove my point. The wild similes are simply not there.

In preparation for writing *The Marble Orchard* I concocted a host of new "Chandlerisms" designed to be incorporated into the narrative. I was quite happy with them; they seemed to match the famous Chandler style. Examples:

She was the kind of blonde who sits in your lap while you're still standing up.

His breath was strong enough to stop a horse at full gallop.

The room was as empty as a pimp's soul.

His smile was as stiff as a bishop's collar.

She was a hippy young thing in a swimsuit she almost had on.

Her eyes were hot enough to melt the enamel off a plaster saint.

She was as jumpy as a nun in a bawdy house.

He was as inconspicuous as an alligator in red shorts.

I had dozens of these, all ready to insert into the book. Alas, I couldn't use them; they didn't match the narrative tone or content. Sure, I stubbornly inserted a few, but kept such writing to a bare minimum; Chandler is not Philip Marlowe.

Enough. Just let me add a special acknowledgment to my wife and fellow writer, Cameron Nolan, for her wise and loving counsel, insightful editing, and valued input. Without her, *The Marble Orchard* would be greatly diminished, and I extend to her my heartfelt thanks. I'm very fortunate to have Cam in my life.

She's my Cissy.

—William F. Nolan
West Hills, California

230